IT'S SUCH A SIMPLE CASE . . .

First, Lou Peckinpaugh's partner is shot and killed in a cheap hotel.

Second, his partner's wife tries to shift the blame onto him although she and Peckinpaugh have been lovers for nine years.

Third, a crazy woman meets him at his office and asks him to find her niece, the job his partner was on.

SEE HOW SIMPLE?

Then, a man with a stinking voice meets him in a chic waterfront dive and tells him that the "niece" is really a valuable object and offers to split the proceeds if Lou will help *him* locate it.

A few things like an old sweetheart, stolen documents, anagrams, and eggs mix it all up a little more.

BUT IT'S REALLY SIMPLE, HONEST!

If you don't think so, then just go ahead and read this crazy book, but remember we told you it was SIMPLE, SIMPLE, SIMPLE!

Neil Simon's
THE CHEAP DETECTIVE

Books by
Robert Grossbach

Easy and Hard Ways Out
The Goodbye Girl

Published by
WARNER BOOKS

THE CHEAP DETECTIVE

A Novelization by
ROBERT GROSSBACH

Based on the Original
Screenplay by
NEIL SIMON

WARNER BOOKS

A Warner Communications Company

WARNER BOOKS EDITION

Copyright © 1978 by Neil Simon
All rights reserved

ISBN 0-446-89557-1

Warner Books, Inc., 75 Rockefeller Plaza, New York, N.Y. 10019

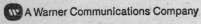 A Warner Communications Company

Printed in the United States of America

Not associated with Warner Press, Inc. of Anderson, Indiana

First Printing: June, 1978

10 9 8 7 6 5 4

For my dear mother-in-law, Pearl.

THE
CHEAP
DETECTIVE

I

DiMaggio was irritable. It was two a.m. on a chill, foggy night and he'd been snugly tucked away in headquarters when the call had come in. Multiple homicide in a cheap hotel down by the waterfront. Get there right away. He'd smashed down the receiver. How the hell did they expect him to complete his report on the Rosen kidnapping when they kept giving him new assignments? The Rosen case at least had been interesting—the wealthy butcher's mother held captive in an abandoned Howard Johnson's, the ransom finally paid in the form of ten thousand pounds of meat-for-chopping since Rosen was short of cash—but this, this sounded like the usual Oriental atrocity story. Why must the Chinks kill each other at two a.m., thought DiMaggio. Why can't they be like normal people and do their murdering before midnight?

9

He put down his pen, stretched, and stood up. He buckled on his shoulder harness and spun the barrel of his .38 before holstering it. He yelled across the room, "Hey! Yo! Crosseti!"

"Yeah, Lieutenant?" came the response.

"Get a car, we're goin' out."

"Right."

Crosseti left the room. DiMaggio flipped the page on his desk calendar to the next day, September 3, 1940, then opened up a drawer and grabbed a bag of salted nuts. With this job, you took pleasure where you found it.

In the car, he offered some nuts to Crosseti.

"I can't," said Crosseti. "Can't have the salt. Blood pressure. Doctor says no salt."

"You got blood pressure?"

"Yeah," said Crosseti. "I got the pressure. Was perfectly normal till about six months ago. Then, one night I go bowling, I miss a spare, an' I go crazy. Angry, you know. Went to the doctor next time, he says 'your pressure is stuck high.' So now I take treatment."

"You mean he gives you drugs?"

Crosseti made a turn. "Nah, nah. I go to his office, see, an' he's got a miniature bowling alley set up there. I shoot spares an' he arranges it so the pins always fall. He says that's the only way to make me cure, you know? To go back to the cause."

DiMaggio popped a cashew. "Sounds reasonable," he said.

They pulled up in front of a cheap hotel, which they identified by the blinking, neon "Cheap Hotel" sign. Two police cars and an ambulance were already there. DiMaggio and Crosseti got out of the car. In the distance, the Golden Gate Bridge shone eerily through the fog. Three uniformed policemen restrained

10

a small, mixed crowd of Orientals, seamen, and bums. DiMaggio extracted a nut and headed for Sergeant Rizzuto, whom he'd spotted at the hotel's entrance.

"What have we got?" he asked Rizzuto coldly.

"Brazil nut, I believe, sir."

"No, no. I mean here."

"Oh, here. Well, here we got someone who's pretty good with a silencer. There's four bodies in there."

"Human?"

"What?"

"All human beings? I mean no goats, or yak bodies, or anything like that?"

"Oh, no, sir. Human bodies. Three of them as cold as yesterday's toast, the last one's ready to pop up."

DiMaggio flipped the Brazil into his mouth. Rizzuto, who'd secretly been practicing that maneuver with scant success, watched enviously.

"Let's have a look," said DiMaggio.

In the lobby, a horde of policemen, hospital attendants, and reporters milled about. The interior was worse than seedy; "decrepit" would've been a step up. The carpet, the nicest part of the room, smelled of urine and vomit and was in shreds. The furniture seemed to be random piles of lumber with nails protruding.

"*Guide Michelin* gave this two holes," commented DiMaggio as he and Rizzuto pushed their way through to the front desk. It wasn't until a flashbulb went off that DiMaggio perceived the first victim. The desk clerk. Male Caucasian, about forty years old. He was sitting comfortably on a stool, a telephone in his left hand. His mouth was open, as if he were in the middle of a word. Features calm, natural, undistorted, except for a small hole exactly centered in his forehead. There was just the barest trace of blood.

"Shot clean as a whistle," said Rizzuto. "He was dead two minutes before he stopped talking."

"Who was he calling?" asked DiMaggio.

Rizzuto opened a small notebook and consulted one of the pages. "City morgue. We figure he saw the bullet coming."

DiMaggio flicked an almond into the air and caught it on his tongue.

"Number two's in the elevator," said Rizzuto, tight-lipped.

They crossed the lobby to the elevator. A uniformed cop stood in front as Rizzuto, DiMaggio, and Crosseti entered the car. Standing up, near the corner, was the operator. Male Negro, about sixty, one hand on the gate, the other on the operating lever. Smile on the face, neat, bloodless bullet hole in the forehead.

"Whoever did it shoots fast," said Rizzuto. "He didn't even have time to fall down."

"Never saw a dead witness who could identify you," said DiMaggio. "Where's the others?"

"Scrubwoman on the third floor, and a guest in three-oh-six."

DiMaggio nodded to Crosseti. "Let's go."

Crosseti looked at the elevator operator. "Three, please."

DiMaggio stared at the ceiling. "We'll walk."

They took the stairs, DiMaggio fielding three peanuts and a filbert by the third landing. They pushed open the heavy stairwell door and stared down the corridor. Two policemen stood guard over a white-sheeted bulk on the floor as the three detectives approached.

"Let's have a look, boys," said Rizzuto.

One of the policemen gingerly lifted the sheet. On her hands and knees was the dead chambermaid. She was looking up, a questioning, surprised expression on her face, when the bullet struck. Dead center on her forehead. As if someone had measured with calipers, thought DiMaggio. A half cigarette dangled from the maid's mouth.

12

"We think the bullet entered her skull, deflected, and came out her spinal column," said Rizzuto. "We couldn't bend her. Probably have to bury her like that."

"Pretty strange deflection for a bullet," commented DiMaggio.

"We checked her medical records," said Rizzuto. "She had a metal plate in her head."

"War wound?"

"No, it was a voluntary operation. She worried a lot about fractured skulls and just wanted to strengthen hers."

"How long she been dead?" asked DiMaggio.

"Since eight o'clock this morning," said Rizzuto.

DiMaggio looked puzzled.

"Same thing for the desk clerk and the elevator operator," continued Rizzuto. "None of the guests noticed it because the service was *always* lousy." He snapped his fingers, and one of the uniformed cops threw the sheet back over the scrubwoman.

"Number four is in here," said Rizzuto.

They moved down the hall to an open door, room 306. One policeman stood outside; another was visible inside.

"This is the joker they were really after," said Rizzuto.

They entered the room. A dresser with a mirror stood against one wall, the bed against another. The carpet made the one in the lobby look plush. The dead man sat in a half-collapsed armcair. He was dressed in a dark brown double-breasted suit. Male Caucasian. Mid-forties. Drink in one hand, newspaper in the other, legs crossed. In his forehead was another perfect bullet hole. The light from the flashing sign outside blended eerily with the room's own illumination, provided by a single forty-watt bulb.

"Some drunk across the hall found him," said Rizzuto. "The drunk thought he was in France. Came in and talked in French for about an hour, noticed he wasn't getting any answers, then switched to English for another hour. When he still didn't get any answers, he got scared."

"And called the cops?"

"No, he went back to his own room and took a bath. Then he got out an Italian dictionary and came back here. By that time he was cold sober and so it only took a half-hour before he realized something was wrong. That's when he called the cops."

"Who's the stiff?" said DiMaggio.

"Floyd Merkle. Runs a two-bit detective agency on Third and Bulldyke. Partner's name is Lou Peckinpaugh."

DiMaggio nodded wearily. Look at him, he thought. Dead at three a.m. in some ninth-class flea-bag hotel. Rigid as a board in roach city. Probably tracked down a million guys cheating on their wives, a million husbands fleeing alimony. A grubber, we got here. A digger, a plodder. He popped a pecan.

"You live cheap, you die cheap," he sneered.

Rizzuto fished in his pocket and came out with a wallet. "Found this on him."

DiMaggio examined it. "Haven't seen one of these in years. A man's wallet, with a change purse in it. I thought they only had these in Poland."

"And what do you think was in the wallet?"

"The Indian Ocean," said DiMaggio. "How the hell would I know? What?"

"Fifty-two thousand Chinese yen," said Rizzuto slowly.

Crosseti whistled.

"Save your whistle," said DiMaggio. "That's a dollar forty American."

"Well, it's still something," said Crosseti valiantly.

14

"Looks like he was set up," said DiMaggio. "Guy like this makes a zillion enemies."

"What?" said Rizzuto. "We didn't see any equipment. No rubber bags, no nozzles, no hoses. Nothing."

"What the hell you talking about?"

"You said," repeated Rizzuto, "a guy like this makes a million enemas. You need apparatus to make enemas."

"Enemies!" shouted DiMaggio. *"Enemies.* He's in a dirty business, people hate him. Now it looks to me like a setup. Whose room was it?"

"Whose room? Whaddaya mean? It belongs to the hotel."

"Who was registered here?"

"Oh, the registry. It was registered to an Oriental, checked in Wednesday."

"Got a name?" asked DiMaggio.

"Name was Wun Fat Ching."

Crosseti began to laugh. "Wun Fat Ching. Jesus, that's funny! That's some hilarious name. Ha, ha. Wun Fat Ching."

"Well, maybe he thinks Crosseti is a big joke, too," said DiMaggio. "Any other information?"

"Only his home town," said Rizzuto. "Registered it as Pecan, China."

"You mean Peking."

"No, Pecan. Like the nut. Sounded like a phony to me, so we looked it up in an atlas. Turns out it's the fifty-eighth largest city in Szechuan province. Five million people. Principal industry is reclaiming old dental x-rays."

"And that's all you know?"

"We know he stayed in his room during the day. We have affidavits from the laundress, a bellboy, and the concierge."

"A place like this has a concierge?"

"Actually, he's a wino, hangs out in the lobby," said

15

Rizzuto. "But he sees everyone who comes and goes. He volunteered the information freely after we worked him over."

"If he didn't come out of his room all day, what did he eat?" asked DiMaggio shrewdly.

Rizzuto flipped open his notebook. "Ah. Good. We checked that. Called the deli across the street and asked for chicken soup with matzoh balls to go. Asked them to leave out the MSG, the NFL, and the DNA."

"Proves nothing," said DiMaggio. "No one can eat Chinese food seven days a week."

"Well, that's it," said Rizzuto. "No other leads, except for one unimportant, though interesting tidbit. Merkle's partner Peckinpaugh was having an affair with Merkle's wife. Saw her two, three times a week."

"Uh-huh," said DiMaggio. "Anyone know for how long?"

"About an hour each time. They used one particular motel where—"

"No, no, I mean how long had the affair been going on?"

Rizzuto squinted at his notebook. "According to the guy in the motel, at least nine years. He says he thinks Peckinpaugh wasn't even shaving yet when they started. That may've been a joke, sir. I cautioned him about further displays of humor. Anyway, Merkle here never caught on."

"Hell of a detective," said DiMaggio, shaking his head. "I wouldn't hire him to find warts on a frog."

A uniformed policeman rushed in then and addressed himself to DiMaggio. "Found two more stiffs next door, Lieutenant."

DiMaggio looked up slowly. "That's the trouble with hotels. Everybody checks out at the same time."

The four men walked out into the corridor.

"Elderly couple," continued the officer. "Moved in last night."

16

DiMaggio nodded. "Tell me, officer, why in your opinion do you think they were killed?"

The policeman's face went blank. "Gee, uh, could be anything. They could've been mob bosses, heroin smugglers, cattle barons, runaway accountants—"

"Or?"

"Or they could've been just plain old people . . . oh, wait . . . plain old people who happened to have heard everything that went on in the next room."

"Now you're cookin', sonny," said DiMaggio.

They entered the doorway adjacent to 306. There, kneeling on the bed, both with their heads and ears pressed to the wall, were an elderly man and woman. The man wore boxer shorts and a torn, sleeveless undershirt; his bony arms and legs protruded like Tinker Toys. The woman had thick, braided hair wound in a knot on her head; she wore a long, gray flannel nightgown. Their eyes were wide open, and a look of keen interest was frozen on their faces. Neat, perfect bullet holes were centered in each forehead.

"If they had a radio to listen to, those two kids would be alive today," said DiMaggio.

"Someone should invent a really small, cheap portable," said Rizzuto.

"Let's go," said DiMaggio.

"Back to the station house?"

"To the Widow Merkle. Now's the time for a visit."

It was a six-story apartment house in a working-class neighborhood. The lobby compared favorably with that of the hotel, although it was inferior to the average midtown men's room. There was no elevator, and the three detectives had to walk up five flights. The staircase, from floors two through four, was unlit.

"I think I stepped in something," said Crosseti.

"What?"

"I dunno. Feels squishy."

"Let's hope it was a banana. Or a pile of noodles. I don't feel like cleaning the squad car again."

They reached the fifth floor and walked down the hall to apartment 5-C. DiMaggio knocked softly. No answer. He knocked a little louder. Nothing. He rang the bell. After a moment, an old woman opened the door.

"Don't you ask who it is before opening?" said Rizzuto.

The woman slammed the door. From inside, they heard a muffled "Who is it?" An eye appeared in the peephole.

"Police, ma'am, open up," said Crosseti.

"Let's see your badges."

One by one, the men held them up to the peephole.

"How do I know those are real?" said the voice. "You could've had them made."

"Ma'am, it's all right now, would you open up? We have some news about your husband."

"Ezra? Don't tell me he's still making those dirty movies. I told him, you want act—"

DiMaggio interrupted. "Mrs. Merkle, may we talk to you inside, please?"

"Merkle?" said the woman. "I'm not Merkle. Merkle is apartment five-oh. Is that who you're looking for?"

"We're terribly sorry, ma'am," said Rizzuto. He turned to DiMaggio. "The O in my notebook looked like a C. I never learned to make certain letters properly."

"Is that what you woke me for?" yelled the old woman from inside. "Is that why you got me out of bed? Well, fuck you where you breathe, lousy cops."

They walked to apartment 5-O and knocked on the door. A woman's voice answered immediately. "Yes?"

"Are you the Widow Merkle?" said DiMaggio.

The peephole opened for an instant, followed by the door. A dyed blond stood in the doorway, dressed in

18

a robe very open at the neck. She tilted her head and placed a hand on one hip.

"Widow Merkle?" said DiMaggio. "Police."

"Georgia," said the woman. "Like the state. I gather my husband's been dispatched."

"May we come in?" said Rizzuto.

"And how did you know," said Crosseti, as they entered the apartment, "about your husband's death?" His eyes narrowed. "There's been no newspaper reports yet, nothing even on the radio. So how could you have known?"

The three sat on a large couch in the living room. Georgia sat on a chair facing them. The apartment had three small rooms, cheap, but comfortable.

"Your partner's use of the term 'widow,'" said Georgia, "simply led me to assume. I mean he said, 'Are you the *Widow* Merkle?' rather than 'Are you the shepherd Merkle?' or 'Father Merkle.' The terminology was the clue. Also, I didn't say my husband had died. I said, 'I gather he's been dispatched.' Now Floyd sometimes worked as a bus driver, so it was a logical inference. Gentlemen care for some coffee?"

"Thank you," said DiMaggio. "I'll have mine black, no sugar."

"Make mine sugar, no milk," said Rizzuto.

"I'll just have some milk with a little sugar in it," said Crosseti. "No coffee."

She stood in the kitchen and worked briefly over the stove before reappearing. She hugged her robe tightly around her.

"Your husband *is* dead, Mrs. Merkle," said DiMaggio. "He was found tonight in a hotel with a bullet in the head."

"The bullet caused his death?"

"We'll have to check with forensic, but we're going on that assumption. A second assumption is that you were involved somehow with the death."

19

"Well, I was married to him."

"No, no, I mean that you helped *cause* the demise. Would you like a moment to get your bearings?"

"No, I have them," said Georgia. She pursed her lips. "Why do you think I'm involved?"

"Well . . ." said DiMaggio.

"It's because of your husband's partner," said Rizzuto.

DiMaggio gave him an annoyed stare.

"We think," continued Rizzuto, "that Peckinpaugh was porkin' you."

"Peckinpaugh was porking me?" said Georgia. "Is that dirty talk for 'seeing me,' or 'having an affair'?"

"We interviewed the man at the motel where you'd been going for nine years."

"But we used false names," said Georgia. "We registered as Mr. and Mrs. Paughkinpeck."

"We have people who spot those things," said Di-Maggio. "Anyway, what have you got to say for yourself?"

"Can I have a hot chocolate instead of the sugared milk?" said Crosseti.

"Of course," said Georgia. "Yes, Lou and I were seeing each other, perhaps even 'porking' occasionally as you so charmingly put it. But no, I did not kill my husband. I wouldn't do that. Couldn't. Besides, there's a clause in his life insurance policy that cuts me out if I murder him."

"And what about his partner, then?" persisted Di-Maggio. "Could he have killed your husband so that he could finally have you to himself?"

"I don't know," said Georgia. She smiled alluringly. "But it wouldn't hurt to ask."

II

He was in a deep sleep, dreaming of toads. The toads were walking in a parade, some of them carrying tiny musical instruments, as they marched through a lightly wooded terrain. Suddenly, the one with the triangle began making a tremendous racket, seemingly gone into a frenzy with the instrument. "Hey!" shouted Lou in the dream. "Hey, you! Knock it off!" The chiming continued. Lou reached out for the berserk trianglist —and woke up.

The phone was ringing. Sleepily, he reached over and grabbed up the receiver. "Yeah?"

"Lou?"

"Yeah."

"It's Georgia."

Lou shook his head. "Oh . . . hello, Georgia . . . I just had you on my mind. What's up, kid?"

"Floyd is dead," said Georgia urgently.

Lou sat up and tried to clear the cobwebs. He reached with his hand near the headboard and swept a few of them away as a large black spider skittered up the wall. Lou grabbed his Mauser pistol from under the pillow and pointed it at the arachnid, but then thought better of it. He reached around to scratch the back of his neck, irritated by one of the twenty-seven laundry tags still on his undershirt. He pointed the Mauser at the phone as he spoke into the mouthpiece.

"Say that again," he ordered.

"Lou? It's Georgia."

"No, after that."

"Floyd is dead. Shot in the head."

"Where?"

"I told you, in the head."

"No, where is he?"

"Oh, Chinatown. I talked to the police, Lou. I think they know about us having an affair."

Lou scratched his head. He was a short man with a tough, narrow-eyed, lined face and a gravel voice. He had a heavy beard and a great deal of body hair. Once, as a joke, he'd shaved the hair on his stomach so that it spelled the word "nop." "But it's not even a word," Georgia had protested when he'd shown it to her. "Well, I meant to write 'no parking,' he'd explained, "but I ran out of room." He thought back now to all the years he'd spent with Floyd, all the cases. They'd had a few good times together. Like when Mrs. Fuller-Richmond had paid them off in trade over a three-year period for not telling her husband when they'd found her in bed with a dwarf headwaiter. Or when they'd finally solved the rash of mysterious murders of fruit vendors by tracing the killer back to the zoo and showing that Ricky, one of the Guatemalan monkeys, was sneaking out nights, commiting a homicide, and then returning to his cage. (The monkey's attorneys had shown extenuating circumstances, resulting in a light sentence.) And all the time, almost from the beginning, Lou had been seeing Georgia. Screwing his partner's wife, while Merkle remained blissfully innocent. Or was he? Had he known all those years? Actually, wouldn't it have been impossible for him *not to know?* It didn't matter. For Merkle, it was all over.

"When did the police leave your apartment?" said Lou into the phone.

"They didn't," said Georgia. "They're standing right next to me now, listening."

In Georgia's apartment Crosseti, DiMaggio, and Rizzuto all put their heads close to the phone.

"Jesus!" said Lou.

"I loved him, Lou," said Georgia. "You know I loved Floyd."

"I know, angel." Lou relaxed his grip on the Mauser.

". . . almost as much as I loved you," continued Georgia. "You killed him because you were crazy about me, didn't you, Lou?"

Lou again pointed the pistol. "Did the cops hear you say that?"

Georgia looked at Rizzuto and DiMaggio, who nodded yes.

"They said yes," said Georgia.

"Don't call me any more, Georgia," snapped Lou. "I don't think we're good for each other." He hung up. His head was spinning and he felt like a drink. He opened up his night table drawer, removed the shot glass already filled with Crème de Cacao, and downed it in a single gulp. The phone rang just as he replaced it.

"I'm sorry, doll," he said, "but certain levels of stupidity are simply not—"

"Mr. Peckinpaugh?"

It took him the better part of ten seconds to assimilate the fact that the voice was not Georgia's but some other woman's.

"Yeah?"

"Mr. Peckinpaugh, I think I have some information regarding the untimely death of your partner, the late Mr. Nerkle."

"Merkle," said Lou. "Who is this?"

"Never mind. As the Chinese say, 'I think I'm being watched.' "

"All right, it's your nickel, as the French say."

"Can we meet in your office in fifteen minutes?"

"All right . . . fifteen minutes. What time is it now?"

There was a mad chuckle from the other end. "Oh no. No information. I'd rather not tell you that until I know I can trust you. And now, as the Italians say, goodbye."

There was a click and the phone went dead. *"Arrivederci,"* muttered Lou, and hung up. From the bottom drawer of the dresser, he grabbed a glass of beer, took a swig, and then replaced it. He climbed off the bed, walked over to his closet, and opened the door. Several thousand moths flew out to greet him. He looked inside. The camphor balls he'd bought last week were gone, eaten by the moths. Soon, he thought, it will be time to move. He dressed quickly, selecting assorted, shleppy-looking, ill-tailored clothes from his vast collection. He put on his black shoes with the tape on the soles.

Downstairs, he hailed a taxi.

"Private Detective Center," he told the cabbie.

They started out.

"You a dick?" asked the driver.

"Uh-huh."

"How's that, a good job?"

"Not bad."

"Pay more than four thousand a year?"

"If you work at it."

"Yeah, that's what I was tellin' my son," said the cabbie. "He's tryin' ta choose a career, somethin' that'll get him inta the big dough, ya know. Somethin' wit' a future."

"Uh-huh."

"That's why he was innerested in drivin' a hack, like me, but I tol' 'm, why not become a private eye. Those guys really rake it in, ya know."

"How old is your son?" asked Lou.

"He's six," said the driver.

"Can't start too early," said Lou.

They pulled up in front of the building and he paid the driver, then got out. The streets were deserted, and Lou went quickly inside, taking the elevator to the ninth floor. He walked through the corridor, his footsteps reverberating against the empty walls, his shadow huge and catlike in the dim cast of the blue night-lights. Finally, he reached his office, "Peckinpaugh and Merkle" stenciled neatly on the door glass. He had just removed his key from his pocket when he noticed the door was already slightly open. He drew his Mauser, then quietly slipped inside. The outer office was dark, and it took nearly a minute before he could make out his secretary's desk and the two small file cabinets. He pushed cautiously ahead, across the room, until he came to his own office, also pitch black. He nudged open the door, and moved slowly forward. His finger rested firmly on the trigger, and he held the Mauser close to his gut. He walked over to his desk . . . and switched on the lamp. An involuntary gasp escaped his lips as he saw the body.

She was a woman of about thirty-five, slumped backwards in the chair alongside his desk. Her head lolled to one side, her mouth and eyes still wide open. Her lipstick looked scarlet in the yellow light, and her lips and jaw were a little too large for her to be called pretty. Actually, she looked somewhat Neanderthal, although her expensively tailored dark suit tended to mitigate the impression. Lou spotted a purse on the floor and retrieved it. He lit up a Camel, inhaled deeply, and swept his gaze around the rest of the room. Nothing unusual. He dumped the contents of the purse on his desk and began his inspection. Lipstick, eye shadow, passport, keys, string, pamphlet entitled *Build Your Own Urinal*, small can of Liquid Wrench, eyeglass case, and a package of breadcrumbs. Suddenly, the woman jerked upright.

"Oh, I'm sorry, I must have dropped off."

Peckinpaugh breathed deeply. "Jesus, that was some sleep you took there." He shook his head. "*Jee-sus*, I'm glad you spoke up. I was just gonna arrange to have you buried."

"I haven't had much sleep lately," said the woman. She began smoothing her hair and clothes. "I've been under a great strain."

"Oh. Yeah, uh-huh. Yeah, a strain."

"I don't suppose you have a drink?"

"Dry martini?"

She nodded. "Mmm."

Lou reached around and opened his middle desk drawer. "Olive or onion?"

"Onion, please."

He closed the middle drawer and opened the bottom drawer, left side. He removed the martini-with-onion and handed it to her.

She sipped slowly. "Thank you."

"My pleasure."

"You're the first one who's shown me any kindness since I arrived in San Francisco."

"And when was that, Miss er . . . ?"

26

"Manderley. Denise Manderley. Two days ago from Shanghai."

"Ah, yes, Shanghai. Been there many times." He narrowed his eyes. "It's particularly nice in the spring, when the *dem sem* blossom, don't you agree?"

"Oh, yes. Quite," said the woman. "May I have my things, please?"

Lou picked up her passport from the top of his desk. "I see you're not a U.S. citizen?"

"I spend a great deal of my time abroad," said the woman, "and most of the rest in New Jersey. Actually, I travel under a Danish passport."

"Really? This passport is Hungarian."

She looked at him then, the tiniest flicker of surprise crossing her face. ". . . yes, Hungarian. They sound so much alike. It's just that the shape of the passport reminds me of a piece of Danish."

"Under occupation it says 'Widow.' "

"That's correct."

"Widow is not an occupation," said Lou, cannily.

"It is when you've buried four husbands."

Lou sucked at his Camel and squinted hard at the passport. "I think I'm getting a little astigmatism," he said. "This signature looks like it's been tampered with."

"You ought to see an ophth—ophth—"

"You're spitting on my desk. Yes, this signature has definitely been retouched. Your name isn't Denise Manderley, is it, Miss Manderley?"

The woman lowered her gaze. "No. It's Wanda Coleman."

Lou picked up a card lying on top of a pocket comb. "Then why does your driver's license say Gilda Dabney?"

The woman blinked seductively. "You're a very sharp detective, Mr. Peckinpaugh."

"It had nothing to do with sharpness," said Lou. "It was a matter of reading. Being able to read is part of my job."

The woman's voice grew intense. "I believe my life is in danger, that's why I've taken so many precautions. My real name—"

"Don't tell me Dabney, the license expired in nineteen-oh-eight."

"My real name is Chloe LaMarr."

Lou put out his cigarette. "Thank you, Miss LaMarr. I appreciate your honesty."

"Honesty is the best policy," said the woman.

Lou fingered a key that lay near the passport. "You believe that, Miss LaMarr?"

"Yes, yes I do. Unless you sell annuities, of course."

"Of course. Well, since we're being honest here, and open, how about telling me why you let yourself in with this passkey and searched my office. What was it you were looking for?"

The woman squirmed in the chair. "To be perfectly frank, your bathroom."

"I don't have one."

She crossed her legs. "I found that out just a little too late."

Lou nodded, and scratched his head. He held up a small handkerchief. "All right, can we stop playing games now? It's not Manderley or Coleman or Dabney . . . or even LaMarr, is it?"

"If you don't succeed at first," said the woman, "try, try again. Genius is one percent inspiration, ninety-nine percent perspiration. When the going gets tough—"

"The initials on this handkerchief," said Lou, "are A. P. What does A. P. stand for? And don't tell me you got it at the A and P."

The woman looked around nervously. "Alma Chalmers."

Lou crashed his fist down on the desk. It was a fist not to be trifled with. Also a desk not to be trifled with. The edge of his hand hurt like the dickens. "Chalmers begins with a C," he said through tightly clenched teeth. "This is a P." Now his teeth began to hurt like the dickens.

"Palmers," said the woman quickly. "Alma Palmers."

"Listen," said Lou deliberately. "You give me the runaround one more time and I'll slap you around this office." He tried to tell himself to relax, but he wouldn't listen. "I don't care what your name is any more. Just make up one so I know what to call you."

The woman sized him up carefully. She'd been correct. A precise, cataloguing mind. Uncomfortable with the slightest uncertainty or imprecision. Fundamentally fearful and insecure. Four more names should do it. "Call me Vivian Purcell," she said.

"That's better," said Lou.

"Carmen Montenegro," said the woman.

Lou rose up menacingly before her. His hands were curled into tight fists.

"You would hit a woman?" said the woman.

"I *prefer* women," said Lou.

"All right, that's the last one, then. I promise."

Lou sat down on a corner of the desk. He smashed the other fist against the top.

"Don't be cross with me, Mr. Peckinpaugh. Now, more than ever, I depend on the gentleness and understanding of strangers."

"What do you know about Floyd Merkle's death?" asked Lou.

The woman looked at the ceiling. "Nothing, of course. Why should I?"

Lou got up and paced around the office. "Did you call me about fifteen minutes ago?"

29

"Yes."

"Did you tell me you knew something?"

"A woman knows many things."

"About Floyd Merkle's death?"

"I don't think so. Why would a woman know that?"

"Then why did you call me?"

"I didn't think *you* would call *me*."

"Why would I?" said Lou exasperatedly. "I didn't even know you."

"Aha!" said the woman. "But you know me now. Life is a circle, as the Chinese say."

"You've lived in the Orient long?"

"The Orient? Naw. I've never been there."

"Then," said Lou shrewdly, "why did you agree when I said the *dem sem* blossom in the spring in Shang—what?"

"I've never been there."

"But you *said* you just came from Shanghai."

"Yes. It's a Chinese restaurant on Redwood Street. Frankly, I'm getting a little tired of their menu, but the take-out place won't deliver, and they're in a neighborhood that—"

Lou was shaking his head. "I mean there hasn't been one true thing about you yet. For all I know, you aren't even a woman. For all I know, you aren't even here. Wait, maybe that's it. Maybe that's it. Maybe I'm dreaming you up."

"Could I have a little fresh air, please?"

"Why? You're only a figment of my imagination."

"Please, I'm feeling dizzy."

Lou stared at her, then crossed to a window and opened it. He looked down into the street. Near the lamppost, a figure stood in hat and long overcoat. His posture was slouched, as if he'd been waiting for some time. He looked upward, toward Lou's window.

"Is that any better?" said Lou.

"Yes, thank you. I'm afraid I got sick all over your filing room in there." She pointed to a door.

"That's the clothes closet. What kind of a sickness was it?"

"You know . . . upset stomach."

"Oh God, not . . . number two."

"No! Course not! A little upchuck, that's all. Some reverse food."

"Oh, okay. That, don't worry about. Go on."

"I have a young niece, Caroline."

"You *are* an actual person, then, as opposed to an apparition in one of my dreams?"

"Yes, a person. My niece is seventeen and attends boarding school at the Hail Mary Sister Theresa Convent and Kennels."

"Kennels? Isn't that for dogs?"

The woman nodded sadly. "I'm afraid none of the girls are very pretty. Two weeks ago, she climbed over the wall and disappeared. She hasn't been heard from since, and I've been worried sick. She could've been abducted and done God-knows-what-with. Raped, sodomized, tortured, forced to eat food with preservatives, given tuba lessons, anything is possible. Since then, I've been frantic. I hired Mr. Merkle to find her. He called me tonight."

"Did he say anything?"

"Yes. He said, 'Hello? Carmen? This is Mr. Merkle.' "

"What about after that?"

"No . . . he didn't say 'after that.' "

"I mean did he say anything else?"

"Yes. He said he had a lead, as you thumbshoes call it."

"Gumshoes!"

"What?"

"*Gumshoes*," repeated Lou. "Not thumbshoes. I be-

31

lieve the expression derives from a private detective's doing so much walking that he often gets gum on his shoes, not to mention shit."

"How embarrassing," said the woman. "I kept calling him a thumbshoe."

"Better than shitshoe," muttered Lou.

"Anyway," continued the woman, "he said he was going to meet someone at this Chinatown hotel with information."

"When was he going to meet them?"

"Tonight. They were supposed to tell him about Priscilla."

"Wasn't her name just Caroline?" said Lou. "I thought her name was Caroline."

"She keeps changing it all the time," said the woman. "It drives me insane."

"That accounts for it," said Lou. "Did she have anything of value on her?"

"I believe she had large boobs."

"No, no. I mean like diamonds or jewelry or soybeans?"

"She had . . . golden hair," said the woman wistfully, "but I don't think that's what you mean, either."

"No, I don't." He lit up another Camel, failing to offer one to the woman. This case was like all the others, unique, skimpy, suggestive of more than met the eye. "It's not much to go on . . ."

"It's all I know."

"I'll do what I can. As for my fee, I'll settle for whatever you owed Merkle. It's only fair."

"It's a lovely gesture," said the woman, "that you won't regret. How loyal you are. I'm sorry I went pookey pookey on your trench coat."

Lou inhaled. "Part of the game. It's happened before." He shrugged. "Look, you must be tired. Why don't you run along now and I'll call you as soon as I get anything."

"I've moved to the Fairmont. I'm registered as Diane Glucksman." She rose from the chair.

"Yeah, well," said Lou, "don't change it again. It makes it hard leaving messages."

The woman moved a step closer to him. She had large brown eyes and a mole just above the corner of her mouth on her left cheek. Her nostrils were flaring. "You're so positive about things, aren't you?"

"I know my stuff," said Lou. "Been in the business for years. I also know my limitations. It's as important to appreciate what you can't do as what you can."

"I can't knit," said the woman, "or filet a fish."

Lou nodded. "I wouldn't worry much about it."

"You don't know what a comfort it is to find someone I can depend on," said the woman.

Lou tilted his head. "How do you know you can depend on me?"

"I just know. Like I said, a woman knows many things. I can see it in your face, your eyes, your hair, your teeth, your lats, your giant *fluvia centralis*." She moved up another step.

"That's very kind of you to say that," said Lou.

"It's been five years since I've known what it is to be even *this* close to a *real* man."

"Five years is a long time. Sixty months. Two hundred sixty weeks."

"Plus a day. There's a leap year in there."

"Plus a day."

"A woman could go quite mad," said the woman. "Meeting all those fake men. Plastic dummies in department stores, three balls of snow and a broomstick, a rented tuxedo draped over a coat-tree. You know the kind of thing I'm referring to."

The woman is undoubtedly clinically insane, thought Lou. Dementia was written all over her.

"It's been a very *lonely* five years," she continued. Her lips were only inches from his.

I wonder if insanity is catching, thought Lou.

"I don't think I'm unattractive, do you, Mr. Peckinpaugh?"

"I have a lot of glands in my body that agree with you."

"We want to keep your *fluvia centralis* healthy, don't we?"

"Yes. Yes, it's one of the things I think about."

"Help me, Mr. Peckinpaugh."

"Call me Mr. Peckinpaugh—I mean, Lou."

"I can be grateful in so many ways," continued the woman, placing a hand on his arm. "Ways you never dreamed of. . . ."

Lou's head swirled with spilled bagfuls of children's toys, plastic automobiles, windblown spirals, endless boxes of gorilla masks, dripping, syrupy things, chocolate gooey marshmallow, the woman lying naked on top of him, giant, sweaty, hairy parts filling his nose and mouth and eyes and ears with her insane essence.

"I'm not asking you, I'm begging you," she said.

"No need to beg," Lou whispered.

"You will help me, won't you . . . Lou?"

Lou closed his eyes and extended his face forward in order to kiss her on the lips. He kissed, noting the strange feeling of her. Her mouth was not open, and her lips felt hard, slightly calloused even. He tentatively extended his tongue, but the lips would not part. He opened his eyes and looked down, discovered he was kissing her finger, which she'd interposed between them.

"Why do you make love with your finger?" he said.

"Sorry," said the woman, with high-school-type coyness. "No helpee, no kissee."

"You jest."

She smiled wanly, turned, and walked to the door.

34

She blew him a light kiss with her hand, then turned and left.

"Terrific," said Lou, aloud. "Maybe Merkle was the lucky one."

III

The Follower got off to a bad start. The youngest boy in the family, with four older sisters, he believed he was a girl until the age of twelve, when he began to shave. His mother, active in civic affairs, and his father, who had four jobs, had never taken the time to correct the misimpression. "I thought it was cute," his mother explained to a city councilman, years later, after the Follower's third arrest. "I would've told him myself," said the father, "but I was always late for my job in the shoe store."

The Follower himself was traumatized by the discovery, realizing he'd missed years of Little League baseball, rolling in dirt, fighting viciously on the school bus, setting fire to cans of hairspray, and all the other male pre-adolescent pleasures and privileges. He had no friends who were boys. His trousers zipped on the side. He was mentally prepared for menstruation. He studied himself in the mirror, looking for cleavage. He borrowed Mommy's lipstick and rouge. He had the world's largest clitoris. The Follower became angry.

He catapulted into puberty with a vengeance. At age thirteen he had a full beard and mustache. He trained himself to urinate standing up. He went from sweet, gentle, and cooperative to sullen, violent, and withdrawn. He beat up all his old girlfriends. His handwriting became sloppy. He threw out all his dresses (except one). He was called in by the school psychiatrist and interviewed.

Psychiatrist: Tell me, Leona, is something bothering you?

Follower: My name is Leon.

Psychiatrist: Leona, I have your records right here. The name on the records is Leona. These go all the way back to kinder-kindergarten.

Follower: My name is Leon.

Psychiatrist: All right, tell you what. I'll call you "Leon" if that's what you want. How's that?"

Follower: (No answer.)

Psychiatrist: Leon, why did you attack Mary Lou Smarm?

Follower: (No answer.)

Psychiatrist: Was it because she reported you hanging out in the men's room, Leon?

Follower: (No answer.)

Psychiatrist: Leon, you must talk to me if we're to communicate.

Follower: (No answer.)

Psychiatrist: Did you go into the men's room because of your beard, Leon? Do you feel closer to men than women?

Follower: (No answer.)

Psychiatrist: You know hair alone doth not make a man, Leon. Many women suffer from excess facial hair, and there are many new techniques for removing it. Electrolysis, for example. Have you heard of electrolysis, Leon?

Follower: (No answer.)

Psychiatrist: Leon, this is the fifth girl you've attacked this month. It simply must stop. You've got to start behaving like a young lady.

Follower: (Unbuckles belt, drops trousers and shorts, exposing himself.)

Psychiatrist: (Calmly.) All right, Leon, enough. I see your point. Yes, that's a more unusual problem for a girl to have, but medical science will soon be able to cope with that, too. Now you've got to—

At this point, the Follower left the interview. In the years that followed, he became progressively bitter, resentful . . . and confused. He dropped out of school and spent time in both men's and women's gyms, lifting weights and removing sightly and unsightly flab. He wore boxer shorts over panty-hose. At age fifteen, he moved out of the house and earned money by mugging. He was overheard to tell a friend, "It's not much, but it's a living." He began a lifelong pattern of assault, alternately raping men and women, which made it difficult for the police to discern either a *modus operandi* or a *lupus americanus*. Sometimes, dressed as a woman, he'd attack a man; then, dressed as a man, he'd attack a woman. Or dressed as a woman, he'd attack a woman. Or, dressed as a wolf, he'd attack a sheep. By age twenty-one, he was a hardened criminal, and a tired one.

Gradually, he became known to figures in the Mob, who used him on odd assignments.

"We wanna you to a-rape the girla frien' of this-a hot-a shot new D.A.," a Capo might tell him. "But just a warning, you capish? Just a-rape her a little."

"I understand," Leon would say, going out then, following the girl, then following instructions.

His reputation grew with both the police and the underworld. His responsibilities branched out from simple rape assignments to carefully controlled and orchestrated attacks. He became expert at committing assault without battery. He acquired an assortment of handguns, hatpins, and attractively embossed sterling silver knives. Once, he bludgeoned a man unconscious with a set of Corning Ware. He lived in a small apartment not far from the railroad station. The walls were blue, the ceiling pink.

It took Lou about twenty minutes to wash all the vomit off his coat. When he was finished, he slipped it on, locked the door of his office, and took the elevator to the ground floor. He lit a cigarette in the lobby before plunging out into the night. He looked across the street from his building, scanning the area near the lamppost. Empty. No one there. Lou tossed away his match and began to walk. Suddenly, he heard footsteps behind him.

Lou smiled to himself and kept walking, increasing his speed. The pace of the Follower quickened as well. Lou stopped; so did the Follower. Lou started again, and so did the trailing footsteps, each a tiny bit closer, a tiny bit louder. Lou began to run, his soles slapping on the empty night pavement. The Follower ran behind him, easily, neither gaining ground nor losing it. Lou had a bizarre idea then, and decided to give in to the impulse. He slowed down and began hopping on one foot. Sure enough, he heard hopping sounds behind him. Lou decided to drag one leg . . . and heard another dragging leg twenty paces to the rear. Lou did the opening of a short tap dance routine from *Peter Pan*. The Follower closed the routine just as Lou ducked into an alley and flattened himself against a wall.

The Follower ran past the alley, then stopped and looked around. He dug his hands into the pockets of his ankle-length overcoat, fingering the twenty-two separate handguns he always carried. The feel of the barrels and the triggers gave him a sense of security. Suddenly, Lou stepped out.

"Can I help you, son?"

The Follower turned quickly. "Uh . . . got the time?" He was flustered, unsure.

"No," said Lou. "Have you?"

"Yeah," said the Follower. He withdrew his hands from his pockets then, and four guns came out with them, and more began falling from the bottom of his coat. Barettas, Mausers, Derringers, forty-fives, bazookas, anti-tank weapons, recoilless rifles, the supply seemed endless.

Lou shook his head. "You must be one of the world's foremost creeps," he said. "An industrial-strength psychopath." He raised his arm, and a taxi pulled over. Lou got in, and the cab squealed off.

Leon the Follower bent down and started picking up his guns. Pockets must've ruptured, he thought. Someone had to pay for this. He decided to rape the tailor.

Lou left the cab, unlocked the door to his apartment, and entered the living room. Georgia Merkle paced back and forth near the window, puffing nervously on a cigarette. She was dressed entirely in black: shoes, stockings, dress, fur piece, and veil. Lou closed the door loudly behind him.

"If it isn't the Widow Merkle," he said coldly.

She turned then, and moved over to him. "Don't be angry, Lou. I had to see you."

"I'll bet."

"They brought Floyd's body home. I just couldn't sleep in the same bed with him, not tonight."

"You've made the funeral arrangements?"

"Yes. It was nerve-racking. They gyp you right and left. The cemetery insisted he be buried in a coffin, and the undertaker insisted he was out of cardboard ones and that all he had was pine. Do you know how expensive pine is these days?"

"I haven't priced it lately."

"Well, it's totally outlandish. I offered the body to medical science, but they have more than they need and won't take a cadaver unless it's in perfect condition. I tried filling the bullet hole with some Plastic Wood, but they spotted it."

Lou studied the ceiling. "Georgia, you must bury the poor man. If you want, I'll—"

"I finally decided on cremation. See that? There's a neat solution to everything."

Lou looked her over. "You are some sweetheart," he said. "A real cupcake, you. Your husband's dead a little over an hour, and you're already in black? How long have you had that outfit waiting in the closet?"

Georgia shook her head. "You're wrong. I just bought it."

"Georgia," said Lou, "will you come on? I mean who do you think you're dealing with here, hah? It's three-thirty in the morning. How the hell you gonna find a store open at three-thirty in the morning? Unless you're tryin' ta tell me you got that outfit at an all-night diner? Is that it?"

"Not an all-night diner," said Georgia, "an all-night widow shop. There's one on Fifth and Geary. Very

42

chic. People die at all times of the day, they've gotta be ready." She moved close to him. "Aren't you gonna kiss me, Lou?"

"Not right now," said Lou. "Look, you shouldn't have come here. The police already think I killed Floyd to clear the way for you and me."

He paced nervously around the room. He had to plan what to do if the cops came. He thought of hiding places. The kitchen sink was too small, under the bed too obvious, in the refrigerator too cold. The closet was out of the question. Too dangerous—the moths would strip him bare in seconds. Perhaps a disguise. He could pose as a plumber, or carpenter. But not at this time of night, he reminded himself. Who *was* up at this hour? Milkmen and private detectives. He would disguise himself as a private detective, he decided, since he had no milk. He turned again to Georgia.

"Are you sure the cops didn't follow you here? Did you take any evasive actions?"

"Like what?" said Georgia.

"Like entering an all-night movie and exiting after a half-hour through a side exit? Or driving across the bridge to Oakland, then doubling back? Or stopping off and refusing to answer questions before a select Senate subcommittee? Anything like that?"

Georgia shook her head no. "But I'm sure the cops didn't follow me."

"How can you be sure?"

"Because . . . they came with me."

At that moment, Lieutenant DiMaggio and Sergeant Rizzuto emerged from the kitchen, and Crosseti came out of the closet. Crosseti's clothes were half eaten away; parts were torn to pieces.

"This is definitely our last date," said Lou to Georgia.

"What the hell you keep in that closet?" asked Crosseti. trying to replace a piece of tattered shirt.

"It started in Rio, I think," said Lou. "Some biologist crossed a moth with a piranha. Now, I hear they're coming up from South America, moving northward at a rate of about seventy miles a year. Killer moths."

"But these are already here!" said Crosseti.

"I was in São Paulo last year," said Lou. "Must've picked up some larvae. Supposedly, they live on second-rate clothes. They choke on any suit costing more than fifteen bucks."

"Lou," said DiMaggio, "we have a few questions we'd like to ask you." DiMaggio studied him. He looked somewhat familiar. They might've seen each other in the halls of the county courthouse. Might've even said hello. The guy had been in the business for a long time; he'd be crafty, and tough to nail.

"You could ask," said Lou, "but I'm not sure I'll do any answering."

"We could go downtown," said Rizzuto.

"We *are* downtown," said Lou.

DiMaggio let that sink in. "Then this'll be fine," he said after a moment. "Lou, Floyd Merkle was killed this evening at eleven-seventeen."

"What street?"

"Wha?"

"You said eleven-seventeen. That's the number. Now I'm asking what street."

"Oh. No, eleven-seventeen was the *time*. Where were you then, Lou?"

Lou thought. "I was home in bed."

"Is it your testimony that you were home in bed then?" asked Rizzuto.

"It's what I said," said Lou. "Although . . . wait. At about eleven-fifteen I woke up and went to the john. I was in there until eleven-twenty."

"Anybody see you go into the bathroom?"

"Yes. There were about seven or eight people who

came in one at a time to watch me. I have their names and addresses on a pad."

"May I have the pad?" asked Crosseti.

"He's being sarcastic," said DiMaggio.

"Is it your testimony that you were in the john at the time of the murder, then?" asked Rizzuto.

"To the best of my recollection," said Lou.

DiMaggio munched on a walnut. "Were you wearing a watch, Mr. Peckinpaugh?"

"When?"

"When you entered the john at precisely eleven-fifteen."

"To the best of my recollection, no."

"Then how could you pinpoint so accurately the times of your entry and exit from the room?"

Lou paused. "May I consult with counsel?"

"You're directed to answer," said DiMaggio, menacingly.

"There's a clock in the bathroom," he said.

With a hand motion, DiMaggio directed Crosseti in to check. Crosseti emerged an instant later and nodded. Lou could see the disappointment pull down like a shade over DiMaggio's face.

"I rigged it up myself," said Lou. "Everytime I flush the toilet the clock gets wound. I prefer watching it to reading. I find it soothing."

Rizzuto had sidled around behind Lou and now, suddenly, he leaned over Lou's shoulder blades. "Don't press your luck, Shabbes."

"You mean shamus," corrected DiMaggio. "Shabbes is the Jewish Sabbath."

"All right, don't press your luck, Sabbath," said Rizzuto.

"Get him off my back," said Lou.

DiMaggio motioned with a hand, and Rizzuto got off Lou's back.

"What did you and Merkle argue about last Monday night?"

"How'd you know about that?" asked Lou.

"A woman knows many thing," said DiMaggio.

"What does that have to—" He looked over at Georgia and suddenly understood.

"Tell them, darling," said Georgia.

"Don't call me darling in front of the police with a dead husband," said Lou.

"Then tell them my big woolly teddy be—"

"Georgia!"

"My ookiepoo-lammie-snook—"

"I didn't like it that he was taking on clients without telling me," said Lou. "That's not how we originally agreed to conduct the business. It was a joint venture."

"That means they ventured into joints," mocked Rizzuto.

"That's what I told them, Lou," said Georgia. "I didn't mention about him busting in and finding us with the Zinc Ointment and the gorilla masks."

"Honey," said Lou, "why don'tcha go in the kitchen and bake a couple a dozen doughnuts?"

"Make mine chocolate," said DiMaggio.

"I'll have sugar," said Rizzuto.

"I'll just take some sugared chocolate," said Crosseti. "No doughnuts."

"What case was Floyd working on?" asked DiMaggio.

"Pillow case," said Lou.

DiMaggio glared at him.

"How about . . . pencil case?"

DiMaggio took a step in his direction.

"Only kidding," said Lou. "Actually he was trying to find out who shot Cock Robin."

"Can you describe this Cock Robin?" said Crosseti. "And where was he shot?"

DiMaggio cuffed Crosseti then with a right hand. "I think your body is making high blood pressure in your torso and extremities and zero in your brain. Cock Robin is not a real person."

"All right," said Crosseti. "No reason to get upset. We've dealt with aliases before."

DiMaggio turned to Lou. "I'm warning you. You withhold anything from me, and you'll be giving the Golden Gate Bridge a new coat of paint with your tongue."

"You hear that, Sabbath," chimed in Rizzuto. "You're gonna be tonguing your coat right there on the bridge."

DiMaggio stalked across the room and left, followed by Rizzuto.

"Forget about my sugared chocolate," said Crosseti, following. He slammed the door.

Lou looked over at Georgia. He lit up a Camel. "Nice pals you brought with you. You sure they're all gone?"

"I think there's one more behind the curtain," said Georgia.

A uniformed patrolman stepped out from behind the curtain. Sheepishly, he tipped his hat and headed for the door. "Sorry ma'am," he said. "Just chasing a speeder on a motorcycle. I tracked him up the steps, but he eluded me at the landing."

"But you're on foot," said Georgia.

"That's why I lost him," said the cop, closing the door.

Lou went to his end table drawer, took out a second Mauser, and began to load it.

"You're going out on that case, aren't you?" wailed Georgia.

"No," said Lou, "I'm just planning to shoot some cockroaches."

"Oh, Lou, come away with me tonight. We can move someplace where the fog never rolls in and a man can see what a woman looks like in the morning."

He pushed her away and continued loading his gun. "I have no desire to live in Bensonhurst," he said. "Besides, being a private eye may not be much, but we *do* have a code of honor."

Georgia guffawed. Then she belched, hiccupped, and spit up.

"Stop guffawing on my couch," ordered Lou.

"It's just that you're so hypocritical," said Georgia. "I mean you talk about a code when you and I have been seeing each other for nine years. I'd like to see that code."

"You wouldn't understand it," said Lou. "The code is in code. But what it says is that it's all right to fool around with your partner's wife so long as the party of the first part shall not be deceased. Upon the partner's demise, or loss of mental competency, or failure to stop a hacking cough within ten days, such fooling around shall be deemed 'dirty' and all the heirs and assignees of the lessee shall grant the aforementioned easements to the lessor, who will then issue a writ of certiorari." He buttoned his coat. "That's the way it is, angel."

"Isn't the lessor required to post bond?" asked Georgia. "Said bond to be held in escrow until an audit is completed of the lessor's estate? I'm just asking."

Lou shook his head. "Poor, naïve Georgia. You marry yourself a nice guy and have a couple of swell kids. Once you're all set up and happy, maybe we can fool around again."

"Guys like you all end up the same, Lou," said Georgia.

"Not me. I'm different."

"No, Lou. No different. You're so busy chasing after runaway girls and missing husbands, you never stop long enough to find out what life is really all about. One day I'll see your picture in the papers laying in the gutter with a bullet hole in your back and a horse making doo-doo all over you—"

"Or vice versa," said Lou.

"Or vice versa," continued Georgia, "and I'll cry for you, Lou, I really will."

Lou looked at her and pressed his lips together.

"So long, baby," she said tenderly. "You're the best guy I ever cheated with." She walked out the door, fighting back tears.

From the hallway, Lou heard very faintly, ". . . except possibly once, that time in Vienna . . ." And then no more.

Suddenly, the phone rang. Lou picked it up. "Yeah?"

The voice on the other end was foreign, nasal, and whiny. It was as if Peter Lorre was having an asthma attack in a sewer.

"Don't heng op!"

"I didn't even say hello," said Lou.

"I know where the girl is."

"Keep talking. Your voice is music to my ears." Much more of this, and I won't have ears, thought Lou. This kind of speaker made you envy the deaf.

"Ohhhh, so now you're interested, heh, heh, heh!"

"Who is this?"

"Let's just say," said the speaker, "it's someone with a high, nasal, obnoxious voice."

"If you've got something to say, squeaky," said Lou, "you'd better say it."

"Not on the phone," said the man (if it was a man). "Meet me at Nick's place on the waterfront in a half-hour."

Lou conjured up a mental picture. He knew the place well, a smoke-filled, cheap dive, packed to the brim with riffraff. A dangerous place where people had disappeared, been knifed, been shot, been sold insurance. "How will I know what you look like?" asked Lou.

"I'm short and greasy," said the voice. "And I wear cheap perfume. You'll smell me as you come in."

"That could describe half a dozen guys," said Lou.

"All right, I also have a mosquito bite over my left eyelid."

"Who doesn't?"

"Six fingers on my left hand."

"That cuts it down somewhat."

"And a grey hair in my left nostril."

"I think that'll do it. Suppose I say I'm not interested, though?"

"Does fife hundred dollars interest you?"

"Very much."

"Then bring it," said the voice. "It's an expensive restaurant."

Lou heard a click on the other end. "Hung up," he muttered.

"No, I didn't," said the voice. "I just clicked. Now I'm hanging up." There was a second click, and the phone went dead. On impulse, Lou smelled the receiver. He reeled back in disgust. Either his ears badly needed a cleaning, or else vinegar and onions could travel over the phone lines.

IV

The doorman was six foot six and weighed two hundred sixty-five pounds; he wore Moroccan garb, including a real scimitar and fez. His name was Hassan Al-Fatah, and he was Irish. He opened the door for a well-dressed young couple who'd just pulled up in a limousine.

"Top o' the evenin' to ya," he said, as the couple swept inside.

Slummers, he thought. The filthy rich seein' how the other half lives. Well, in there they'd get a small taste. And if he were nice to them, said a few words to them as they left, possibly they'd throw him a buck or two. Long ago, he'd swallowed his pride. The idea was to accumulate money, and he'd lower himself to any depths in order to further his ambition. One day they'd see his name on Park Avenue in New York:

Hassan Al-Fatah, *Floral Arrangements to Go*.

Inside, the cabaret was in the usual turmoil. Smoke from cigarettes combined with various male and female scents and the aromas from drinks to produce a near-unbreathable mixture of gasses. Two overhead fans turned with extreme and useless slowness, their main effect being to distribute the noxious fumes evenly about the room. The place, Nix Place, as the tawdry neon sign announced out front, attracted all kinds. French army officers mingled with deposed Arab sheiks who rubbed elbows with Norwegian sailors who stood next to Eurasian hookers who solicited watered drinks from Hong Kong businessmen who were trying to pick up cosmetics heiresses. In the center of the room, at a white upright piano, wearing a white dinner jacket, was a black, prone man who sang while he played. Every few minutes he'd right himself and sit properly on the bench, before sliding inevitably back to the lying position. In a corner, a roulette table was going full blast, five-dollar minimum wager, with plenty of bettors interested in the action.

Nearby, at a chair positioned against a side wall, Marcel, the manager, kept an eye on things. He was a well-built man with a mole on his right cheek, a lengthy nose (good for humming patriotic songs through), darting eyes, and a mouth that twitched occasionally. He inhaled a Gauloise as one of the dinner captains whispered softly in his ear.

". . . just phoned," said the captain.

"What?" said Marcel. "Lean closer, I can't hear."

The captain brought his lips close to Marcel's head. "The German Embassy just—"

Marcel jerked his head away. "Not that close! You're licking my ear!"

"The German Embassy just phoned," said the man, embarrassed. "Colonel Schlissel would like dinner at his usual table tonight."

Marcel balled his fists, squeezed the fingers till the knuckles were white. "The pig!"

"No," said the captain. "He said he wanted roast veal."

"Very well," said Marcel, resignedly.

"No," said the captain. "He ordered it medium."

"All right!" said Marcel, the anger rising again. "All right, I understand! And tell the Colonel I have a special treat I think will please him."

The captain nodded and walked off.

Outside, a cab pulled up to the curb. Lou got out, paid, and was heading toward the front door when someone called his name. He strained, but could see nothing in the nighttime blackness.

"Lou!"

He turned, and managed to discern a familiar face. Out of the shadows near the side of the building, the man limped in his direction. The limp was a most unusual one, alternating from one leg to the other as follows: three limps on the left, and pause, two, three, then one on the right, two, three, and back with the left, two, three. Lou recognized it as an old Peruvian dance, the *chambo*. The figure approached more closely and other details became evident: the filthy white trousers, grease-stained, striped pullover shirt (some of the stripes were actually stains), the battered, soiled yachting cap. And the incessant scratching. The man scratched everywhere as he limped, a kind of syncopated motion that seemed almost part of the walk. He scratched his week-old beard, his underarms, and his legs. He stopped about a foot away.

"Hello, Lou." He scratched his chest. "I been waitin' fer you, Lou. Just like I said I would."

Lou eyed him benevolently. He tried to suppress the immediate kindly thoughts that entered his head: thoughts of riddling the old man with bullets, or running away and jumping into a hot bath. "Hello,

53

Hoppy," he said. "I thought I saw the last of you in Cuba."

Hoppy picked his nose. "Not me, Lou. I swam back after the boat blew up."

Lou remembered the situation. He'd been working on special assignment for the CIA, trying to blackmail a KGB agent who'd been sent to Havana on the QT to organize a militant rally of BAGS, the Bra and Girdle Sewers union, whose members also assembled parachutes. The KGB man was known to have a secret sexual preference for older women who got frequent headaches, and Lou had managed to arrange an offshore yacht party to which the Soviet agent was invited, along with several Hadassah groups. The small boat to ferry the agent out had been rigged with explosives, of course, and one expendable, filthy old salt.

"Shark bit off my kneecap, Lou," continued Hoppy, "but then he gagged and refused to eat the rest of me. Checked into a hospital soon's I made it back to the beach, but my Blue Cross plan didn't cover this kind of injury. I had the three-star Better Benefits arrangement, and the best they could do was give me some string and tell me how to tie up the knee." He slapped himself hard in the forehead. "Darn mosquitos."

"How'd you know where to find me?" asked Lou.

"Oh, you know. Usual ways. Just went through the phone books of every major city in the U.S., Canada, Europe, and South America."

"My number's unlisted."

"That's why it took so long," said Hoppy. "Listen, I told you I'd be around when you needed me. You're workin' on a case, ain't you, Lou?" He ducked then, and a huge horsefly buzzed over his head. "That one had my number on it. Those things get any bigger, we'll need air raid shelters." He hunched his shoulders.

"I sure could use a drink, Lou. My string hurts awful bad."

Lou nodded, and reached into his pocket. He did, after all, owe something to the man. "All right," he said, "but this is the last one." He brought out a mint julep, not spilling a drop, and handed it to Hoppy, who immediately gulped half of it down.

"Thanks, Lou."

Lou waved and resumed walking toward the entrance. Hoppy *chambo*-limped after him.

"Hey, Lou . . . do you know why a bumblebee buzzes?"

Lou instantly recognized their old pass code. "Because the beating of his gossamer wings creates a longitudinal wave disturbance in the air which acts as an elastic propagation medium?"

"Nope."

"Because certain instinctual reactions are triggered by a release of hormones into his circulatory system, the buzzing being a way of provoking interest from the female?"

"Doubt it."

"Because . . . he doesn't know how to knock."

The old man hopped up and down gleefully and did a one-and-a-half full gainer from the pike position. "You remembered, Lou. Gol dern it, you remembered." Lou thought he saw a tear run down Hoppy's nose, but changed his mind when the tear ran back up again. "You're okay, Lou."

Hoppy launched into a little dance then, a *hora* to the tune of "Some Enchanted Evening." Hassan Al-Fatah, the doorman, came over and grabbed him by the shoulders, then pushed him aside.

"Get away from here, you dirty old rummy!" he said in a kindly voice.

Lou, though a good ten inches shorter and a hundred pounds lighter than Al-Fatah, turned and swung, catching the doorman square on the chin. Al-Fatah laughed. "Was that your best?" He advanced menacingly on Lou.

"I'm a fourth-degree black belt," said Lou. "I've studied Tai Kwan Do, Kung Fu, Moo Duk Quan, and Almond Gai Ding. Although it appears I'm at a great disadvantage, it's actually you who doesn't have a chance."

"Where there's life, there's hope," said the doorman, seizing Lou by the collar and practically lifting him off the ground.

Choking, Lou sputtered, "Speak softly and carry a big stick," after which he grabbed a large stick leaning against the wall and swatted Al-Fatah on the head.

The doorman released his grip, then lashed out at Lou's chin with a left hook. "If at first you don't succeed, try, try again."

Lou dodged the blow. "Many a slip between the cup and the lip." He cocked his left leg then, and sent a short, chopping kick to the doorman's groin.

Al-Fatah reeled sideways into a vendor's flower cart. "Your petunias are really coming along," he groaned.

"That's not a saying," said Lou, rushing in with a vicious elbow to the doorman's jaw, which sent him spinning off into unconsciousness. "You talk to anybody like that again, you'll have to bend over backwards to whistle for a cab."

He brushed himself off and turned to the old sailor. "You okay, Hoppy?"

"Sure, Lou. I can take care of myself. You know that, Lou. You don't have to worry about old Hoppy none, Lou. How'd you ever beat that big mother, though?"

"I knew more proverbs than he did," said Lou. He grinned. "Now get out of my way, you dirty old rummy."

56

He gently shoved Hoppy aside and made his way into the cabaret.

"Thank you, Lou. You're a comfort."

Al-Fatah began to awaken. "He who hesitates—" he said thickly. But there was no one there.

Lou walked down a flight of stairs and paused at the bottom to let his eyes, nose, mouth, and ears fill with smoke. Next to him a hat check girl wearing a leotard two sizes too small stood and waited.

"Check your hat, sir?"

"If you say so," said Lou.

The girl stood on tiptoe and looked over his head. "It's okay," she said. "You want me to take it now?"

"Take it whenever you wish," said Lou.

"I'll take it when you give it to me," said the girl.

Lou sniggered as he removed his hat. "I like your double entendres," he said.

"Thank you," said the girl, glancing down at her cleavage. "But I think it's mostly the bra that pushes them up."

Lou handed her the hat, which she stuffed between her breasts. She gave him a small ticket in return. "My number's on the back of the check. Call me when you want your hat back."

"Very tricky," said Lou, entering the club.

The dinner captain approached him. "You're expected, Mr. Peckinpaugh. This way, please."

As they walked past the piano, the piano player spotted Lou. "Hiya, Mister Lou. Long time no see."

"Hello, Tinker. Has she ever—?"

"No, she hasn't."

"Right!"

"Would you like me to play—"

"No!"

"Right."

Lou and the captain walked on. "Your party will join you in a moment," said the captain.

They stopped at a ringside table, where Lou sat down. The captain stood waiting. He cleared his throat.

"You want something?" asked Lou.

"Nothing, monsieur. Only to say that it is customary, upon being shown your table, to respond with a nominal gratuity."

Lou looked at him and narrowed his eyes. "Of course. How gross of me." He reached in a pocket, came out with a small certificate, and handed it to the captain, who examined it.

"But monsieur, this only enables me to get ten cents off on any size jar of instant Maxwell House," said the captain, finally.

"Best I can do," said Lou. He produced a few more pieces of paper and scanned through them. "Unless you want my old library card."

The captain began walking away.

"How about a free month at a health spa if you sign up for five years?" Lou flipped through the papers and yelled louder. "How about directions to my brother-in-law's house?"

But the captain no longer heard.

The three men all wore black tuxedos. Their leader was tall, thin, and severe-looking, with bony features and a monocle in one eye. His gaze was unwavering and took in everything; the stare had the penetrating energy of insanity. The other two men were practically interchangeable, very blond, young, and mean. Their facial muscles tensed into throbbing knots as they came down the steps. Marcel rushed forward to meet them and bowed obsequiously.

"Colonel Schlissel, you do my humble café a great honor."

Schlissel, from his greater height, regarded Marcel

as one might an insect. One of the other men sprayed something in Marcel's direction. "Your little club reminds me of the fighting strength of the French army," said Schlissel. "Nothing more than a night's diversion."

Marcel stiffened with anger and gritted his teeth. He felt an old filling loosen in a rear molar. The Germans chuckled in unison.

"By the way, Marcel," said Schlissel, "would you be kind enough to lift up your trousers for my two hundred percent Aryan friends?"

"The one on the left asked for a bagel when he came in last week," said Marcel.

Schlissel turned to one of the blonds. "True?"

The man straightened and clicked his heels. "*Nein!* He iss lying. Vass not a bagel!"

Schlissel regarded the man coldly. "Vass a bialy, perhaps, hmmm? Ve could make you talk, you know."

The man began to quake. "Ya, vass a bialy," he whispered.

Schlissel addressed himself to the other German. "Ve'll need a report here viss all ze details. If there vass lox or any hint, place him unter immediate arrest. Haf a blood test done for cream cheese."

Both men clicked their heels.

"Now, Marcel, up viss ze trousers, ya?"

"Monsieur?"

"Come, come, don't be bashful, Marcel. Lift up your trousers."

Reluctantly, breathing heavily, Marcel raised his pant legs to the knee. Some day, he thought, I will drown him in piss for this. Some day, I'll force him to eat cold pizza.

"You see," continued Schlissel, gleefully, "you vere wrong. Zey *do* have frog's legs tonight."

The other two Germans chuckled dutifully.

Marcel bit his lip so hard that the tartar came off his teeth. "Oh, you make the little joke, *monsieur*." He quickly rolled down his pants. "Now, if you and your friends will follow me, I will show you to your usual, world-dominating table."

He led them into the smoky club, pushing through the crowd, and finally pausing at a table next to Lou's. Marcel will not forget this insult to his manhood, he thought. As long as he lives, Marcel will remember this. This will stay with Marcel for as long as he refers to himself in the third person. The Germans sat down, Schlissel first, followed by the two others.

"Ve'll haf zum caviar," said Schlissel, imperiously, "und six bottles of Cordon Bleu, 'thirty-four."

Marcel clasped his hands togther. Six bottles of the Cordon Bleu! A small fortune! "Six bottles? Of course! I'll see to it myself."

Schlissel pointed to a man and a woman two tables away. "Und you zee that lovely young couple zeated there?"

"Oui, monsieur," said Marcel, his heart sinking.

"Put it on their bill," commanded Schlissel.

"Of course," said Marcel. The swine, he thought. The worms. That meant they wanted it for free. That he would have to give it away. Marcel will remember this even longer than the frog's leg joke, he thought. He will recall this even *after* he has stopped living. He bowed stiffly and walked away. *"Boche!"* he muttered under his breath, and "Shitheads!" over it.

"What did you say?" came Schlissel's angry voice.

"Nosh!" said Marcel quickly, without turning. "A nosh! A nice little nosh, I'll send it right over to your table."

He hurried away then, perspiring and licking his chin nervously. Several parts of him twitched independently. At that moment, there was a fanfare from the small band onstage. Tinker, the piano player, stood up on his bench and addressed the audience.

"And now, ladies and gentlemen, let's give a nice

San Francisco welcome to Miss Betty DeBoop!"

There was applause, and then the house lights went out, and an arc light illuminated a white, beaded archway near the side of the stage. A hand reached around and pulled the beads aside as Betty DeBoop slunk her way through the opening.

She was a long, slim girl with long, slim legs, long, slim hair covering one eye, and long, slim breasts, most of which were exposed. She'd grown up as Betty Poobed in Atlantic City, New Jersey, quit school when she was sixteen, and begun a promising career as a waitress in a Nedicks. "You're the best orange juice worker we got," the manager had told her after two years, "but you're already at the top salary level for your position." Since the hot-dog making slot was occupied, Betty's advancement had reached a dead end. One day, the manager approached her just as she was heading for lunch. "Hey, Betty," he said confidentially, eyeing the attractive teenager (even then she was long and slim) up and down, "there is one thing you can do to make yourself some extra cash." "What?" asked Betty innocently. Leering, the manager leaned over and whispered in her ear.

A day later, Betty was performing oral sex on an impotent Middle-East potentate. This had nothing whatsoever to do with the manager's suggestion, which involved investing in cattle ranches as a tax shelter, but had resulted from the monarch's offer to launch Betty on a singing career if she'd gratify his desires. The potentate, it seems, could only find satisfaction with teenage waitresses; his fantasies required that they enact a tableau of rude, sloppy service, after which he would have sex with them under a specially constructed counter, shouting at the climax, "You want a tip, I'll give you a tip!" and then falling asleep for seven hours. Betty had the natural instincts and the body to please him perfectly, and it was not long afterward

61

that she was introduced to the Director of Entertainment on the cruise ship *Karpinsky*, a Polish pleasure vessel. The ship was actually a converted explorer, formerly used in an effort to find a water route to Switzerland, now specializing in budget cruises from Staten Island to Brooklyn. "Not bad," said the Director of Entertainment when he saw Betty. "Don't suppose you can sing, can you?"

"I do all right," said Betty, feigning confidence.

"Doesn't matter," said the director. "You got a captive audience here. Where they gonna go, over the side?" And he laughed hysterically. "What's your name again? I always forget names."

"Betty Poobed."

"No good. Gotta change it to something with a ring. How about Betty Ring?"

Betty shook her head.

"How about leaving out part of your last name? Betty Poo. No good. Sounds like you stink. Can't have people thinking you stink. Wait a minute, how about Betty Bed? Yeah, I like it. That's it, Betty Bed. Sexy, unique, suggestive. Perfect."

She sang for two years under the name of Betty Bed, trying out her act, shaping, cutting, improving before her captive audience. She filled out, and attracted many men. Eventually, she met a nightclub impressario who was opening a place in London and needed a chanteuse.

"What're you gonna do, Betty, waste your whole life here on the *Karpinsky*?" he said. "Come with me to Britain, and you can waste your life in London."

Betty accepted. She sang for three years in the Club Homo, a gay bar in the Soho District, which catered to homosexuals in the construction trades. She became so popular that she'd attract a standing-room-only crowd; people in the audience were touched by her delivery and phrasing, as well as by the people next to them. Summers, when the club closed, she'd be booked at places on the Continent. She became familiar with Rome, Paris, Vienna, and Snurtvurst, a small Bavarian town where she performed before a convention of schizophrenic German mining engineers. And all the time, she longed to return to the States.

"I long to return to the States," she'd tell her friend Rudolf, a kindly old man who put taps on shoes.

"So, my child, vy don't you do it?" said Rudolf.

"Oh, Rudy!" she exclaimed, "You're right! Why didn't I see that before? Oh thank you, Rudolf!"

And she did him a small sexual favor involving vaseline and pieces of herring, and then booked passage to San Francisco. A new life requires a new name, she thought, when she arrived. "Who're you?" asked the manager of the first nightclub she tried out for. "Connie Bed," she said. "Very big on the continent."

"Very small here," said the manager when she'd finished.

She went through seven or eight places, bombing out at each of them, and feeling lonely and miserable. Finally, she realized that there was only one difference between her success in Europe and her failure thus far in the States—her name. And yet, she needed something, she knew that, some change to mark off this new stage of her career. How about Betty Failure, she thought. How about a return to her old name, Betty Poobed. Too plain. How about—a lightbulb went off in her head. She replaced the bulb, and suddenly it came to her. Reverse the letters of her last name and make two words out of it. Betty Debo Op.

The manager of the ninth place wouldn't even speak to her. She tried Betty Deb Oop. No good. Finally— a last shot—Betty DeBoop. She opened before a group of longshoremen-with-doctorates-in-city-planning. They went wild. Next came a bar catering to married men too frightened to cheat on their wives. She was a smash hit, booked for ten weeks in a row. Some of the men actually cheated during this time and were tossed out of the club. Finally, a grand opening at the Pervert Room where degenerates of all types could relax in an atmosphere of warmth and congeniality. Naturally, she was a huge success, and it was but a short step to the stage of Nix Place.

She sang in a sexy, husky voice now as Tinker played the introduction to "La Vie en Rose." She used the style she'd developed so painfully through all the lean years on the *Karpinsky* and the ones speckled with ugly fat in Europe. No lyrics. "Never give them lyrics," the manager of the Club Homo had told her. She moved around the room.

"La . . . la la la la . . . la la la la . . . la laaaa. La . . . la la la la . . . la la la la . . . la la laaa . . . la."

She strolled between the tables, stopping occasionally to sit on one, sometimes cradling a man's head in her arms, if convenient.

"La . . . la la la . . . la la la la . . . la la laaaa. Oh, la la la la . . . mmm la la . . . la la la la. . . ."

She came over to Lou and sat in his lap, "La la, la la. . . ." She stuck her tongue in his ear and placed her hand on his thigh. "La la la la, oh, la la . . . mm la la la . . . la laaa."

Schlissel glared enviously as she neared the end of the song and ran back onstage for the rousing finish.

"La la la la . . . la la la la, la *en rose.*"

There was tumultuous, prolonged applause. Several men in the audience fainted (alcoholics), and one woman urinated on the floor (slob). Betty took her bows as Marcel came up behind her and whispered in her ear.

"The Nazis at that table—you see it, in front?— request the pleasure of your company. Better give it, or they'll have you executed."

Betty nodded, took a final bow, and crossed toward

Schlissel's table. Schlissel was standing up, toasting her with champagne. Betty, on the way, stopped near to Lou and removed a cigarette from the pack next to him.

"Hello, Fred," she said. "I was hoping you'd drop in."

"The name is Lou," said Lou, grinning, "and I don't believe we've ever met."

Betty looked down at him. "Let's not get hung up on details, Fred." She leaned over to him and held the cigarette up to her mouth. Important portions of flesh were spilling out of her dress. "Aren't you gonna light my fire?"

"Yeah," said Lou, "I was just looking over your kindling wood."

He lit her cigarette, and she blew out the match. Marcel rushed up to her, feverishly wiping the perspiration off his forehead.

"What are you standing here for? There are three absolutely charming and delightful Nazis waiting for you at the next table!"

"Hold your *pâté de foie gras*, Frenchie," said Betty. "I'll be right there." She turned back to Lou. "If you're not busy, Fred, I get off at two. Don't you think two is a good time to get off on?" She winked at him.

If only I could transplant her body, thought Lou, onto the head of an anthropologist. Or to anyone who spoke reasonably. Or to an inanimate object that at least kept silent, such as an inner tube, or an earring. Why were beautiful girls always so vulgarly stupid? Perhaps it was a natural defense, or perhaps it was caused by too much lanolin in the diet. This would also account for their being sheepish. Betty sidled over to Schlissel, as Marcel followed.

"Gentlemen," he said, "may I present Miss Betty DeBoop. From the Islands."

"Caribbean or Virgin?" asked Schlissel.

Betty smoothed down her hair and thrust out her chest. "Let's just say I came back a Caribbean."

Schlissel threw back his head and laughed hysterically. His face grew florid, and then he began to choke, which he found even more amusing and which caused him to increase his laughter. He began to spit up tiny pieces of his lunch. After ten minutes, he calmed down.

"How delightfully gauche, Miss DeBoop," he said finally. "I've always been enchanted with a lack of breeding."

"And I've always been enchanted with breeding," said Betty.

This set Schlissel off again, laughing and choking, until one of his boots came off and his nose began to bleed. He wiped himself with a handkerchief proffered by one of the other Germans. "Permit me to introduce myself," he said.

"Okay," said Betty, "but make it fast."

"I am Colonel Prince Count Baron Von Schlisseldorf, Germany military attaché to Cincinnati." He rose, bowed, and clicked his heels together (which hurt, since one foot was bare). The other Germans also snapped heels; a shrewd observer would've noticed that the pattern of clicks spelled out an obscene suggestion in Morse code.

"Don't crack your shins on my account, boys," said Betty.

"Please," said Schlissel, "sit down and join us. Ze veal here iss excellent. As is ze knockvurst, ze bratvurst, und ze livervurst."

"How's the chopped steak?"

"Ze vurst—"

"But I'm asking about the steak."

"Und I'm telling you. Ze vurst I've ever eaten. I think zey use balsa vood instead of meat. But now . . . haf zum champagne, und tell us about yourself."

"Nothing to tell," said Betty. "I was born in Atlantic City. Sometimes, as children, my friends and I would walk on the boardwalk as if in a dream. Life was sweet then, all pea—"

"Peas and carrots?"

"Yes. I used to fantasize that someday I'd be a sleazy chanteuse in a tawdry, decadent, San Francisco club and that I'd dine on chopped steak with fascist thugs."

"Und now your dream has come true."

"Fairly close," said Betty. "Say, do the other two Germans ever talk?"

"Only under direct command," said Schlissel, "or severe torture, or when they have to use the men's room. Otherwise, zey are rigged for zilent running. Both are former Y-boat commanders, of course."

"Y-boat? What's that?"

"A Y-boat is a U-boat zat turns back on itself. After an assignment, it's ordered to fire torpedoes at its own hull. A zuicide mission, you might say."

"But how come they're called Y-boats?"

"Because their captains always ask, 'Why?' These two, of course"—he indicated the blonds—"failed to complete their tasks, vich is vy zey are here instead of gathering greater glory for ze fatherland."

"Some people never know when they're well off," said Betty.

Marcel had returned to his chair and was watching the roulette. He sipped some apricot brandy. A college professor had come in and was attempting to win a lot of money using some arcane mathematical formula. He made detailed computations before every bet, and had already amassed ten thousand dollars. He explained the scheme to a woman next to him, and Marcel leaned over to listen.

"It has to do with application of the gamma function generalized factorial to Bayes' Axiom. I discovered one day that the probability distribution, instead of being Gaussian, was actually Rayleigh, if you use the optimal strategy."

"But I've been watching you," said the woman. "You've just alternated red and black for the last two hundred times in a row."

"That's the way it seems to *you*," chuckled the mathematician. "Ah, you laymen," he sighed.

"Sometimes," said the woman. "Tell you what, I'll place a bet exactly like yours. If we win, you come up to my room and I'll show you my theories."

The mathematician placed all his money on the black. The wheel spun, and Marcel leaned forward to watch. "Red!" called the croupier, collecting the huge pile of chips. The professor sat absolutely still for a moment, thinking.

"Stick your gamma functions up your gink!" said the woman graciously. "I lost two dollars."

"I think I forgot a minus sign," said the mathematician.

The dinner captain came over and whispered in Marcel's ear. "They just called from the French underground."

"Collect?"

"What?"

"I said, was the call collect? Because we're not taking any more collect calls. My phone bill last month was over twenty dollars."

"No the call was regular," said the captain.

Marcel looked around nervously. "Quiet, you fool, there are enemy ears all over, many on the sides of enemy heads. Lean closer."

The captain leaned closer and said something that Marcel could not hear. "The garlic on your breath is giving me an earache," he said. "Now just lower your voice, but keep the same distance away."

68

The captain moved his lips, but no sound was audible.

"Still too low," said Marcel, "I can't hear a thing."

"Testing," whispered the Captain, "testing one-two, testing one-two-three."

"That's better," said Marcel. "All right, what is it?"

"The underground has called. DuChard and his wife are on their way here. I tried to stop them, but I was too late."

Marcel nodded. "You understand, of course, that this is why Schlissel comes here every night. Hoping one day he'll get his hands on DuChard. Or his feet."

"I don't think that's completely true," said the captain. "I think he really likes the roast veal."

Marcel turned and looked at the man incredulously. Was it possible he'd had a lobotomy recently? Or had wearing tight collars gradually shut off the blood supply to his higher intelligence centers, leaving him with the IQ of an azalea? It was but another imponderable.

The captain moved over to Lou's table. "Your party will see you now."

"Can't hear," said Lou.

The captain said, "I'm tired of people not being able to hear me."

Lou didn't hear the remark.

The captain grabbed a napkin and scrawled on it with a pencil, "Your party is at booth seven."

"Can't read this," said Lou, staring at the napkin.

The captain wrote, *I'm tired of people who can't read my writing,* but Lou couldn't make out that message, either. Finally, the captain indicated toward booth seven and held his nose.

"Thank you," said Lou.

A waiter emerged from the booth where the captain pointed. He staggered and fell on a nearby table, knocking over a drink. When he righted himself, he apologized profusely. Lou stood up and peered into the smoke. Booth seven was in a dimly lit corner, completely hidden by bubbles, bangles, and bright, shiny beads.

"See you around, Slinky," he said, as he passed Betty DeBoop.

"Just snap your fingers and I'll dump the krauts," said Betty.

Schlissel looked annoyed. Lou smiled and headed for booth seven. On the way, he passed Tinker, still doodling at the piano.

"Hey, Mister Lou," said Tinker, "any time you want me to play . . ."

"I said no."

"Right," said Tinker.

Lou stopped in front of the beaded curtain around booth seven and lit a cigarette. A high, nasal voice came from within.

"Please do come in, Mr. Peckinpaugh."

V

Lou parted the curtains. Sitting there was a small man with a gold earring in his ear, a brightly glittering gold tooth in the front of his mouth, and hair arranged in black, springy curls, some of which were so oily they dripped on the tablecloth. He wore mauve gloves, a velvet suit, and smoked a Turkish cigarette held in a long holder. He looked as if a gypsy king had mated with a floor mop.

"Pepe Damascus, at your disposal."

Lou inhaled and winced. A mixture of gasoline, dog urine, and a sardine sandwich left in the glove compartment of a car on a sunny day.

"I may take you up on that," he said.

"I hope my disgustingly cheap perfume doesn't offend you," said Damascus. "You see, I purposely stink to keep my enemies from getting too close."

"Well, they're better off than your friends are, then."

"Thank you. A seat please?"

Lou sat down, as far away as possible from Damascus without being entirely out of the booth. Damascus dripped on the table.

"Have to change my oil," he said. "In the winter I usually use a twenty weight, but when the warm weather comes around I like to switch to something with higher viscosity. Otherwise, I'm quite reasonable, never use more than a quart every other week." He grinned, flashing the gold tooth. "Someday my hair will be worth a lot of money," he said. "Put my tooth to shame."

"I like your earring," said Lou. "Although I think a smaller hoop would go better with your face. But tell me, you said you knew where the girl was."

Damascus waggled a finger. "You're so impatient, Mr. Peckinpaugh. There are amenities to be observed, haggling to be done, certain items of protocol to be decided. Would you care for some Greek hozzerai?" He pushed forward a plate that appeared to contain the excretions of a small dog.

Involuntarily, Lou drew back.

"Really very excellent," said Damascus. "Made from the leavings of goats who'd been fed the collected works of Turgenev. Some people believe it increases your knowledge of literature."

Lou stared at him. "All right, quit stalling. If you've got something to say, talk fast. Your perfume is giving my nose an extra nostril."

Damascus laughed. "Ha! You are an inventive fellow, and inventive fellows deserve the truth. Very well, there is no young niece Caroline or Priscilla or whatever Mrs. Danvers told you."

Lou shook his head. "She also didn't tell me it was Mrs. Danvers."

"She hired your partner, Mr. Markle, to—"

"Merkle."

"—to find a priceless, missing 'work of art.' Mr. Markle didn't tell you that because he was going to split the money with Mrs. Danvers."

"Talk faster," said Lou. "Your voice is rusting my keys. Really, I can't take much more without medical attention."

"Perhaps," continued Damascus, "she killed Mr. Markle in fear that he would double-cross her."

"That's hard to swallow."

"No harder than the container of lye she poured into my cream soda in Alexandria. In Cairo, she put a live electric wire in my bathtub."

"And you're still here."

"Yes, in a manner of speaking. Course, I used to have straight hair and be six-foot-four. But one must be grateful for even Allah's smallest gift."

Lou narrowed his eyes and nose. "Am I right in assuming, then, you want me to go to work for you?"

"You are indeed a very clever dumbshoe," said Damascus. "Help me recover the missing object, and I shall split a fortune with you, fifty-fifty."

"A split, huh," said Lou.

"Shall we shake on it?" said Damascus. He extended a greasy hand, which Lou just looked at.

"If we split, I want sixty-forty," said Lou. "How can you stand being around yourself?"

"It isn't easy," said Damascus. "No hotel will take me for the entire night. I used to wear a nose clip, but I had 'to give it up when I couldn't breathe. I'm often ejected from busses, and attacked by dogs in the street. The only people that'll speak to me are from computerized dating services."

The beads parted momentarily, and the captain entered their booth. He leaned over and whispered to Lou.

"Pardon, *monsieur,* but there is a message for Mr. Damascus. Would you give it to him, please?"

"Why don't you give it to him?" asked Lou.

"I'd rather not get that close," explained the captain. "I have a date later."

"What is it?"

"Mr. B. has arrived in San Francisco from Jerusalem. He is staying at the Crusades Hotel."

Lou nodded. "All right. I'll tell him."

"Thank you, *monsieur,*" said the captain, "and here is something for you." He handed Lou a small paper and then left.

Lou examined the writing. *Good for one free ride on the merry-go-round, New York World's Fair.* Lou crumpled the paper and put it in his pocket.

"So," said Damascus. "I couldn't help overhearing. At last he's arrived, eh?"

"Who's Mr. B?" asked Lou.

Damascus chuckled. "Jasper Blubber."

Lou coughed. "Please . . . don't chuckle," he gasped. "The fumes . . ."

"Sorry," said Damascus.

"Who's this Blubber?"

"An insidiously dangerous tub of lard. We must move quickly."

"What is this 'thing' you're all after, anyway?" asked Lou.

Just at that instant Damascus whipped out a small, pearl-handled revolver and pointed it at Lou. "I had it taped under the table," he said. "When the captain distracted you for an instant I was able to get it."

"Big deal," said Lou.

"You're too curious, Mr. Peckinpaugh. Curiosity is what killed the putty tat. You will be so kind now as to raise most of your hands."

Lou lifted his arms. "What is this?"

Damascus chuckled. "Let's see, how should I phrase

74

it? Fund-raising? A benefit dinner? Donation to a worthy cause? Hard to say. Anyway, it's a stickup."

"Oh, come on. I thought you just hired me."

"I did. But I also need money badly. It's hard finding a job because of my fragrance. Skunk obedience-training positions are few and far between. Very far. I haven't gotten past a job interview in six years. Matter of fact, they rarely even let me stay to fill out the forms."

"I'm sorry, but I find it difficult to develop any sympathy right now."

"Sympathy I don't need," said Damascus. "Just develop your wallet into my hand."

Lou reached back and extracted his wallet. He flipped it to Damascus. "You won't get far with what's in there. Don't forget, I'm an impoverished private eye."

Damascus pocketed the wallet. "Don't worry about me, I'll get by." He chuckled and stood up. He donned a black overcoat that had been slung over a nearby chair and flung a white scarf around his neck. "If you have to get in touch with me, I'll be at the Carleton Hotel until four-thirty a.m. Then they make me move to the Stratford Arms. A business doing pleasure with you, sir."

He stepped out of the booth. An instant later, Lou attempted to follow, but when he emerged, Damascus had completely and utterly vanished, leaving behind only a putrid smell as evidence he'd been there at all.

Outside the club, a black Renault sedan pulled silently up to the curb. The driver got out immediately and ran around to open the rear door. He was dressed in the outfit of a French peasant. Paul DuChard got out of the back of the car, a handsome, fortyish man with soft features and graying sideburns. In his mouth were two cigarettes, one of which he gave to the driver

75

before reaching back into the car to help his companion. The hand that grasped his belonged to a woman, a brunette in a white tailored suit and matching, wide-brimmed hat. She wobbled unsteadily as she stepped onto the sidewalk.

"Paul . . . are you sure it's all right to come here?" she asked in French-accented English.

"There is nussing to worry about, *n'est-ce pas?*" said Paul. "We are safe now here in England."

"No, Paul," said Marlene. "This is America."

Paul looked around, and shook his head. "Ah, yes . . . America. Land of zee opportunity, *oui?* Land of lakes and azure streams aflowing. Land of milk and honey. Land of zee blind where zee one-eyed man is king. Land where—"

"We should have gone to a doctor, Paul," said Marlene. "I'm not sure zat I got all zee bullet out of your head."

He put his arm around her. "But you studied, *non?* You spent much hours."

"It was only two weeks, Paul, and it was a correspondence course. Zee week before I was practicing giving injections to peaches, and before I knew it, poof, there I was, playing find-zee-fragment in your brain."

Paul kissed both her hands. "It doesn't matter, *chérie.* It's zee thought zat counts." He turned to the driver and kissed both *his* hands. "And now, Michel, drive back to Paris, and God go with you."

"Yes, sir," said Michel. "I'm picking him up in Marseilles."

Michel saluted and got back into the car. Paul and Marlene walked to the entrance of Nix, where Al-Fatah opened the door for them. Just as he did so, Pepe Damascus brushed by Paul on his way out.

"I beg your pardon."

"No, no," said Paul. "My fault."

76

Damascus swept off into the night.

"If this is what America smells like," said Paul, "we should have stayed underground."

Inside, he gave his hat to the girl. Marcel came rushing forward.

"Madame DuChard!" he said, kissing Marlene's hand. He turned to Paul, and they vigorously shook hands. "Paul! It's so good to see you."

Marcel and Paul hugged each other. Then Marcel kissed Paul on both cheeks, and Paul kissed Marcel on both cheeks. Then Marcel kissed Paul on his eyes, his nose, and his ears, after which Paul bent and kissed Marcel's calves, ankles, and feet. Marlene coughed, and the men broke apart.

"I'm sorry, *madame*," said Marcel.

"I understand," said Marlene. "I love him, too."

"I tried to stop you both from coming," said Marcel. "You must leave, Paul. Colonel Schlissel from the Cincinnati Gestapo is here."

Paul nodded calmly. "So. Ze Black Fox has followed me from France."

"And also his assistants," said Marcel, "the Golden Ardvaark and the Spotted Clam."

"Well I am safe as long as I remain here in San Francisco," said Paul.

Marcel leaned close. "But he knows you intend to open a little French restaurant in Oakland," he whispered.

"He knows?" said Paul, the tiniest bit shaken. "How did he discover? Who is ze traitor?"

"They captured one of our men and tortured him for days, forced him to fill out college registration forms while wearing turtleneck sweaters. He gave them your name just before he died."

"Poor fellow. He will go down as a great patriot."

"He already went down," said Marcel.

"The point is," said Paul, "if I do go to Oakland . . ."

"Take one step on the Oakland ferry," said Marcel, "and your life isn't worth two francs."

Paul stiffened. "I have not come this far to be stopped now, Marcel. Maybe in a little while, but not at this time. I have fought long and hard for France. I have sacrificed for the ideals and principles of our nation. I have dedicated myself to continuing the great traditions our forefathers have established."

"And who knows that better than I?" said Marcel.

"*I*," said Paul. "*Moi*. And the job is not done. We need a three-star restaurant in Oakland. A place where all free Frenchmen can gather round the radio and listen to ze war. A place with a ladies' room, and men's room with ze finest, hand-carved urinals. A France away from France."

"Paul is an obstinate man," said Marlene. "Even with a bullet in it, his mind is made up."

"What about the documents?" asked Paul.

Marcel whispered. "Your papers of ownership and the liquor license are to be delivered here tonight. Also, twelve thousand placemats, two hundred dozen napkins, and three rolls of toilet paper."

"The toilet paper," said Marcel, "one side rough, one side smooth as I requested?"

"Yes. If all goes well, you will be ready to offer your first bouillabaisse within thirty-six hours. In the meantime, we must wait."

"Well, as you know," said Paul, "they also serve who only—"

"Make a dollar twenty an hour," said Marcel. "Yes, I know. The old waiter's motto. We expect the courier with your papers at any moment."

He led Marlene and Paul across the room.

"France owes a great debt to you, Marcel," said Paul.

"It comes to a little over fifteen hundred francs," said Marcel, "but we can settle that later."

They passed the piano, and Tinker spotted Marlene. Quickly, he glanced over to booth number seven where Lou was still sitting.

"Oh, oh," he muttered, continuing to play.

At Schlissel's table, one of the Germans spotted Paul and tapped Schlissel on the shoulder. Schlissel was whispering into Betty's ear. "You are as lovely as a Panzer division overrunning Poland, as fragile as a Luftwaffe formation fl—what?" He turned and looked then, squinting so hard that the monocle cracked in his eye socket. He stood up as the party passed his table.

"What a pleasant surprise, *Monsieur* DuChard."

"So," said Paul, "ze Black Fox and ze Silver Wolf meet again."

Schlissel indicated his henchman. "Und, of course, you remember ze Golden Ardvaark und ze Spotted Clam."

Paul nodded curtly. "May I present my wife Marlene."

Schlissel clicked his heels. "How could I forget ze White Swan?" He bowed. "Formerly ze Orange Chicken, vasn't it?" he said slyly.

Marlene gave him a haughty look.

"It is always ze most courageous men who win ze most beautiful women," said Schlissel. "But it is only ze ruthless who get to keep zem."

Marlene thought of all those years in the underground, years of eating souflées that never rose and the binding of books that never sold, years of preparing the giant *crêpes* that were to be flung over the Nazi tanks at the appropriate moment, years of sleeping with creepy German officers to glean a tiny bit of information or a plate of lobster bisque.

"And it is a thousand candles," she said ringingly, "that will burn for every brave soldier that—"

"That's a lot of candles," interjected Marcel. "Couldn't we get the same effect with, say, twenty or twenty-five?"

"—marches to the steps of the drums of liberty so that tyranny will never trample the spirit of freedom in the hearts of men throughout a world thrown into darkness and despair."

Is it possible, thought Marcel, that the bullet has traveled from his brain to hers?

"Well spoken," said Schlissel, "whatever it means." A fanatic after my own heart, he thought. Any worthwhile cause was worth going over the edge for. "May I present Miss DeBoop?" he said, indicating Betty. "Like yourself, a vell-built exile."

Betty crooked a finger. "Hiya, honey. Don't let the Heinie get you down."

Schlissel glared malevolently at Paul. "I hope you plan to stay in San Francisco for a while, DuChard."

"You are enamored of my company, I suppose," said Paul.

"I am suggesting a means a preserving your health. If you tried to leave I vould miss you, but most certainly my two friends here vould not."

Paul smiled. "You forget, I have stared death in the eyes many times, Colonel."

"Und no doubt death has turned away in disgust," joked Schlissel. "Maybe said, 'Who iss this ugly Frenchman dot keeps looking at me? Vot iss he, queer?' "

"And yet," continued Paul, "it is death that wears glasses, not I. Death that has red marks on the bridge of his nose from the pressure of the frames. Death that must be examined twice a year by an optician."

"And a martyr is nothing but a fool who picks up the check every time his country sends out for lunch," said Schlissel.

"And a table," said Marcel, "is but a flat horizontal surface supported at some height from the ground."

"As is a Frenchman," said Schlissel.

"I'd rather be a live coward than a dead hero," said Marcel.

"No, no," said Schlissel, "ze saying is 'I'd rather be a live hero than a dead coward.' That's ze only vay that makes sense, *ja?*"

"And it is the despots and tyrants who run our rivers red," said Marlene. "Red with the colors of a hundred trampled flags that unfurl in the winds of liberty, blowing over centuries of deprivation and—"

"You make no sense at all now," said Schlissel, "although your idiotic ranting is most charming. There are no centuries of deprivation. Ze Third Reich has only been around a few years. There *vill be* centuries of deprivation, but not yet. Also, look at any river und you'll see it never runs red."

Paul put his arm around Marlene. "It's all right, darling, we've made our point." He began to lead her away, but Marlene faked left and turned right.

"And there'll yet be a place where men who have known treachery and treason and the jackboots of a thousand dictators can still light torches that burn with quiet intensity in the hallowed caves of honor—"

"We'll have a drink now," said Paul firmly. "Come, *ma chérie,* we'll see the show, relax a bit. Come, it will calm you down."

"Where our dead shall rise," continued Marlene, ignoring him, "from the graves of our ancestors, striking down the pagan hordes, casting out the corrupt and the oppressors from the temple of earthly domination, and restoring once more the righteous and the good—"

"Why don't we dance, darling?" said Paul desperately. He seized her forcefully by the arm and began to walk. "You used to dance so well before you started making speeches."

Marcel took Marlene's other arm and the two led her to a table. Colonel Schlissel watched them coldly.

"There, gentlemen, goes a brave, beautiful and extremely boring woman," he said to the other Nazis.

Just then, two small men entered the club. Each of them wore a dark suit and hat and had a mustache and darting, shifty eyes. They looked like politicians, or judges, or importers specializing in olive oil. One carried a leather attaché case chained to his waist. He held the case tightly to his chest. The dinner captain met them at the door, nodded without a word, and showed them to a table against a side wall. The men did not take off either their hats or coats when they sat down, but one of them did remove his mustache.

Schlissel leaned over to whisper into Betty's ear. "Do you like chocolate, my dear?"

"Depends," said Betty. "What type?"

"German chocolate," said Schlissel. "Made to rigid specifications. Vill *obey* your mouth, not just melt in it. Much better zan Hersheys."

"Does it come with almonds?"

"*Nein*," said Schlissel. "Ze *Führer* does not permit nuts to spoil ze purity of ze chocolate."

"How about Necco wafers?" said Betty. "Can you get me those?"

Schlissel smiled. It was the same all over. Everyone had his price. Living, all of life, was just a matter of bargaining efficiently and making sure you could get the best deal. A matter of perception, really. Perceiving the vendor, perceiving the customer (yourself), and perceiving the social order. He leaned back. "I vill drown you in Necco wafers, if that is your desire," he said.

"I think seven or eight packs would be enough," said Betty. "Another good thing is butterscotch Lifesavers."

One of the Germans held up his hand.

"Yes?" said Schlissel.

"May I be recognized?" said the German.

"You may," said Schlissel, chuckling, "if your disguise isn't good enough."

The German moved his eyes toward the two men in the corner.

Schlissel addressed Betty. "My friends und I are going to speak in Italian now, Betty. Ve mean no offense. It simply lets us communicate more effectively. You understand?"

"I think you should try Yiddish," said Betty.

The first German whispered in Schlissel's ear. "But I don't know Italian, Colonel."

"Dummkopf!" whispered back Schlissel. "I told her that to throw her off. Of course, shpeak German."

The man nodded, *"Eine kleine* zits shpy kummin, *mein Herr,"* he said aloud.

Schlissel glanced around quickly, then turned back. "Keepen ze eye oppenz fursht." He smiled at Betty. "There, that wasn't so bad, was it?" He grew serious. "Listen, it's possible there could be some trouble, my dear."

"You mean because of the Italian?"

"No, no. Something else. Just remember, if there's any shooting, get under the table."

"That's the first place I'll get into trouble," said Betty.

Marlene spotted Tinker halfway across the room and gasped in surprise.

"What is it, darling?" said Paul. "Why are you gasping in surprise? Have you an orange rind stuck in your throat?"

Marlene shook her head no.

"Did you just dislocate a shoulder perhaps? Or get a sudden hernia?"

Marlene kept shaking her head.

"This thing that surprised you," said Paul, "is it an animal, rather than vegetable or mineral?"

Marlene nodded yes.

"Is this animal more commonly found in the city than on a farm on in the jungle?"

Another yes.

"Is this animal an erect biped, genus *homo*, species *sapiens*?"

Yes.

"Could it be then—"

"I'm sorry, *monsieur*," interjected Marcel, "but our time is up."

"—that you have seen something that reminded you of a long-lost love whom you ardently and passionately desired but gave up because intellectually and philosophically you were more compatible with another?"

"No, Paul," said Marlene.

"And could it be that this 'another' is none other than—"

"We must take a station break!" Marcel practically shouted.

"I merely . . . had a little gas," said Marlene quietly. "A pain that passes like two streetcars in the night. A pain that goes to the depot and is then refueled and overhauled and has new wheel bearings installed. And is then cast out to begin a new journey."

Marcel leaned over to Paul. "You should have her looked at. I'll send you to a good man."

Behind them, the captain was pointing out Paul to the two men seated against the wall. The man with the attaché case nodded vigorously. "So he is the one, eh?"

"Yes, the very same."

"Formidable."

84

Marlene approached the piano player. "Hello . . . Tinker. How have you been?"

Tinker loosened his collar and rolled his eyes. "I don't know no other songs, ma'am."

"None? Nothing by Chopin? Bach? Nelson Eddy?"

"This is the only one I know. One-song Tinker, that's me."

A note of urgency and pleading came into Marlene's voice. "You haven't forgotten it, Finker—I mean, Tinker. You could *never* forget it."

"Forget what?"

"You know very well."

"I can't play it without the music, ma'am. I'm a piano man that needs his music."

Suddenly, a voice rang out from behind Marlene. "Here . . . take mine."

She turned then, and saw him. Lou stood holding out a piece of sheet music, the paper so yellow, faded, and torn it looked like a Dead Sea scroll. "I knew I should have had it laminated," he said. "Hello, Marlene . . . long time no see."

Marlene stared at him, transfixed. "Hello, Lou. No see in long time."

"See time no long," said Tinker.

"How long has it been?" said Lou.

"Since what?" said Marlene.

"Since the price of soybeans rose a dollar a bushel," said Lou, annoyed. "Since what do you think?"

"Since the discovery of a cure for anthrax?"

"Marlene—"

"All right, all right, I'm teasing. I know. Don't you think I know? Since we last met. Early Pleistocene period, wasn't it?"

"Marlene—"

"About three years, I would guess."

"It was two weeks ago Saturday," said Lou. "How quickly you forget."

"Forget what?" said Tinker. "I told you, ι gotta have the music."

"I *know* that, Lou," said Marlene. "Accuracy is not everything here. I am trying to convey a *subjective* experience that has nothing to do with the passage of absolute time in the Newtonian sense. Besides which Einstein showed that absolute time is a myth, anyway, in the famous *gedonkin* of the simultaneous lightning bolts witnessed by an observer who—"

"Marlene—"

"Assuming, of course, that the speed of light is the top limiting velocity in the universe. What I'm saying is that it just *seemed* like three years."

"Then why couldn't you just say that?" said Lou.

"Some of us were blessed with the gift of rhetoric," said Marlene, "and it would be an affront to God and nature were we not to make use of that gift. Also, we can't return it if we have it more than ten days."

"You could exchange it for something useful," said Lou. "Like a pot or an umbrella."

"I'm married now, Lou," said Marlene. "Pots and umbrellas are part of my life. Also, I'm . . . trying to run an underground."

"What? Trying to run under ground? How the hell —you need a bulldozer or—"

"No, no. An underground. Supervising an underground."

Lou nodded, then grinned sardonically. Then he grinned sarcastically and superficially. "Why didn't you tell me you liked heroes, I would have helped an old lady across the street."

She slapped him hard across the face, and he grabbed his mouth. He thought: some people think it's okay when a woman slaps you across the face because women only give weak, feminine slaps that are really nothing more than outward expressions of outraged inner feelings. Actually, they hurt like a sonofabitch

86

and make your face all red and puffy and filled with lymphatic fluid, and women ought to be hit back hard so they'd learn to desist from repeating that particular maneuver. He drew back his hand and suddenly felt a large lump lodge in his throat.

"I swallowed my gum!" he managed to choke out. "I swallowed my gum! You made me do it!"

Marlene watched him and thought back to the time they'd spent together in Paris. Days of idle laughter on the Right Bank, days of busy laughter on the Left Bank, days of idle business in the Chase Manhattan bank, days in Manhattan, the Bronx, and Staten Island, too. Memories came flooding back of night-time strolls along the Champs-Élysées, of *bateaux mouches* along the Seine, of the time she'd accidentally thrown up on Napoleon's coffin and the guard had fined her three francs for "fouling zee tomb." And always him there, with his deep voice and gentle hands, stroking her hair, pausing during a walk to fondle her cheek, ducking under the table at dinner to bite her feet, slipping a shopping bag over his head before they went to bed. She pictured each incident in minute detail, recreating individual episodes like the pieces of a stained glass window, assembled finally like a mosaic, a memorial to their love affair. Parts of a puzzle that was the key to her life, pages in the book of her existence, eggs in the crate of personality, beer cans and used enema bags in a junkyard of discarded dreams. She'd loved him, but he was uncommitted. Uncommitted to anything.

"I want someone who *is* committed," she'd pleaded.

"Try a mental hospital," he'd joked.

"You jest while I pour out my heart. I want someone who believes in something. Who isn't so empty, jaded, and cynical that inside he is but a dried, sere husk that will wither and die. For without commitment,

87

thou canst not relate to the pains of human kind, and therefore, by reflection, to thineself and mineself."

"I don't understand that," Lou had said.

"Because you have no philosophy."

"Because I never took Old English. Why does a Frenchwoman revert to that, anyway?"

"Why? Hah! Why? Thou canst not comprehend, can thy? You were never one for things of the intellect, Lou. With you, it's 'me first.' "

"What's wrong with that? What's wrong with putting you first?"

"No, 'me' first. 'Me' meaning you."

"Did you know Immanuel Kant died a virgin?" asked Lou.

"Too late," said Marlene. "Too late for *non sequiturs* now, Lou. Too late for *ad hominems*. Maybe in time for *fusareum* blight, but that's about all. The Germans are at the gates of Paris—"

"Paris doesn't have any gates."

"Too late for literal interpretations. My heart has gone out to a leader of the Resistance."

"Marlene," he'd choked, "I can lead, too. I can be a leader of Voltage, or Current, or even Kilowatt-hours. Just . . . give me some time."

She'd looked at him with tears in her eyes. "Oh Lou, oh darling, how I wish I could. But the situation is desperate. And besides, he has an eight-inch tongue. But I'll never forget you, Lou."

"You're a real sport," Lou had muttered.

Paul came up behind her now and cut short her reverie, which had run over the allotted reverie time by two minutes and twenty seconds. "Is anything wrong, my dear?"

"He swallowed his gum," said Marlene, indicating Lou. "He suffered a temporary paroxysm."

"My mistake," said Lou. "For a second I thought this young lady was a girl—"

"She is a girl!" said Paul.

"I mean a girl I knew in France."

"You know her?" asked Paul incredulously.

"No," said Lou, "I was wrong. The girl I knew is dead."

"A natural error, *monsieur*," said Paul. "Though a stupid one. My wife has been mistaken for dead girls by many men."

Marcel came up behind Paul and whispered in his ear. "The documents are here," he whispered.

"How?"

"Courier."

"They came by pigeon?"

"No, no, *courier*, not carrier. Small, shifty-eyed men brought them. One of them said he is running for mayor of New York."

Paul nodded and turned to leave. Suddenly, there was a fanfare from the small band on stage. The bandleader raised his hands above his head.

"May we have some quiet, please!"

The hubbub persisted.

"Ladies and gentlemen, please! Please, may I have some quiet!"

There was a slight lessening of the noise.

"Ladies and gentlemen, may I please have your attention! I have an urgent announcement!"

The club fell into a hush.

"The Dodgers have scored two runs in the eighth inning to take a four-to-three lead over the Cardinals. There's been a pitching change, and they're now in the top of the ninth."

A loud cheer, mixed with some boos, came from the crowd.

"Also, this Friday, the Knights of Columbus are holding a singles dansant at the Frisco Town House. This Friday. All medical students will be admitted free, all women, half price."

The audience began to grow restless.

"And last, but not least, we've just received a bulletin over the wireless from the B.B.C. in London."

"What now," said Lou, "the soccer scores?"

"At oh seven hundred hours this morning, word was issued by the new Vichy government that the First German Panzer Division has entered the rue des Castiglione and is now trying to find parking space. It is with deep regret we must inform you—Paris has fallen."

VI

"Paris fell," murmured the audience. "Paris fell. Hey, did you hear that? Paris dropped!"

"The management has requested me to add," continued the bandleader, "that the price of wine must be raised two dollars a bottle. Thank you."

A hush came over the people. Betty stood up and crossed over to stand with Lou. Paul and Marlene joined Marcel and the captain.

"Paris!" sobbed Marcel. "Paris—I cannot believe it."

"Maybe," said the captain, "it's a different Paris."

"I don't think so," said Marcel. "There is only one Paris."

"And as long as there is one Frenchman, one true patriot," said Marlene, "then the Seine shall purify the soiled streets of our great city, and wash clean the wide, tree-lined boulevards and verdant—"

"Oh, please!" said Paul, bitterly. "Nobody wants to hear that crap now. We have lost everything, our homes, our pride, our crêpes. We have nothing now but the flesh on our bones and a few internal organs."

Lou stared disconsolately into his glass. "The fall of Paris always makes me want to get plastered," he said.

Betty touched his shoulder. "Now's not the time for cheap jokes and vicious puns, Fred. I always get depressed as hell when Paris falls."

Lou took her hand and squeezed it.

"Why don't we get out of here, Fred?"

"Look," said Lou, "as far as I'm concerned, the world can blow itself up at nine o'clock tomorrow morning."

"The banks wouldn't be opened yet."

"I don't care," said Lou. "All I want is an eight o'clock wake-up call." He downed his drink, a mixture of vodka and milk called White Christmas.

Suddenly, a rich, tenor voice began to sing.

"Ze eentzie veentzie shpider vent up ze vater shpout . . ."

Marcel looked around. One of the Germans had risen, glass of beer in hand, and had begun to sing triumphantly, chest thrust out, eyes bulging. Within seconds, the other Germans were standing and lifting their glasses, joining the first with immense pride.

". . . down came ze rain und vashed ze shpider out. . . ."

The other people in the club watched them mutely, their faces masks of despair. Suddenly, a lone voice piped up with a counter-song, thin and reedy, but determined. It was Marcel, on his feet, and forcing the words from his mouth.

"Where is thumbkin? Where is thumbkin? Here I am! Here I am. . . ."

Marlene rose to join him. ". . . How are you this morning? Very well I thank you. Run a-way. Run a-way. . . ."

The Germans looked over at them and tried to maintain their chorus. ". . . Out came ze sun, und dried up all ze rain, but. . . ."

Paul and the captain rose to join Marlene and Marcel. ". . . Where is pointer? Where is pointer? Here I am! Here I am! . . . ."

They poured all their emotions into the singing, and soon the Germans, nonplussed, could only stop and stare.

"How are you this morning? Very well I thank you. Run a-way. Run a-way."

There was a hush, and then the audience broke into feverish applause.

"You heard ze last line of ze song?" said Schlissel to the nearest Aryan, as they sat down. "Run away. Zat iss vat zey did, und zat iss vat zese fools are applauding."

"Vas zat song part of ze show?" asked the Aryan.

Just then Tinker began to sing at the piano. "Wind, wind, wind your bobbin. Wind, wind, wind your bobbin. Pull. Pull. Clap your—"

Lou was at the piano in a flash, slamming the keyboard cover down hard and just missing amputating Tinker's fingers.

"I told you not to play that song!"

"I'm sorry, Mr. Lou. I told her you wouldn't like it."

Behind them, the courier with the attaché case crossed over to Paul's table, his aide right behind him. The case was still chained to his wrist, and his aide was attached to his body by a rope that extended around both their waists. The courier leaned over Paul's shoulder.

"Monsieur!"

Paul turned. "Yes?"

"Everything is in order."

Marcel leaned over. "Not here. Give him the papers in the toilet."

The courier nodded and immediately started for the john, jerking his aide along after him. Paul and Marcel both stood up.

"Where are you going, darling?" asked Marlene.

"To the toilet," said Marcel.

"Not you, him!" said Marlene annoyed.

"That is where we are going," said Paul. "For zee papers. It will be all right."

He patted her head reassuringly and left. Schlissel, watching, spoke to his two comrades.

"Go inze both into ze men's room!"

"But, Colonel," protested one of the Germans, "I don't haf to machinze."

"Get!" said Schlissel sternly. "Und bring back ze documents!"

The two Aryans left.

Lou, his arm around Betty, looked over at Marlene. "I must've been crazy fallin' for a dame who wears a hat like that."

"And what's under the hat is a little peculiar also," said Betty.

"Can you lend me a ten-spot?" asked Lou. "I'd just like us to get out of here, Slinky."

"I can do better than that, Fred."

She reached down into her bosom and pulled out his wallet. She handed it to him. "I think this belongs to you."

Lou stared at it in amazement. "How did you—?" He began to leaf through the bills.

"It's all there," said Betty.

"I'm sure it is. The question is how could—"

"I can lift anything you want, including the creases in your pants."

She reached down into her bosom again, this time coming up with a hubcap from an old Hudson and a can of tuna fish. Once more she tried and retrieved a small bowling ball formerly used by Lou Campi, and a pamphlet entitled *Guide to Tax-Free Municipal Bonds.* "Last shot," she said, dipping in and coming up, finally, with Lou's hat.

"Here's your hat, Fred. I'm glad you didn't carry an umbrella."

Lou smiled. "You wouldn't have a spare shoelace in there, would you?"

The Germans waited outside the men's room door.

"Ve give zem a minute," said the taller one. "Zen ve catch zem in ze act."

"Vat act?"

"Ze act. Zere iss only vun act."

"I thought zere vuss two. Vy do zey haf ze urinals, zen?"

"Be quiet!"

Through the door they heard the sound of an attaché case being unsnapped. They rushed in, only to find Marcel undoing the snaps on his pants. Too late. They launched themselves at Paul and Marcel.

"Nazis!" yelled Marcel.

"Take cover!" yelled the courier. Frantically, he tugged at the closed door of one of the stalls.

Paul gave one of the Germans a short, edge-of-the-hand chop across the back of the neck, knocking him to the floor. The German shook his head groggily. "Never hit a Nazi in the neck," he said, rising to his feet.

"Why?" asked Paul.

"Because . . . it hurts!" said the German, flinging himself this time at the courier.

95

With a last bit of strength, the courier managed to rip open the door of the cubicle. Inside, a small man sat reading the *Times*. He stood up as the courier frantically scrambled in.

"Can't get any reading done," said the man, starting to leave without even zipping up his pants. "All I want is five minutes to do my reading, and they won't even give me that."

The German shoved him aside and lunged at the courier. Meanwhile, Marcel had dropped to the floor and, in a move learned from years of studying *savate,* French foot-fighting, was biting the toes of the other Aryan. "Give up, swine?" Marcel screamed.

The German howled.

"Give up?"

"Nein!" said the German.

"What?"

"Zat's *nine* toes you've bitten," said the German, in great pain.

Suddenly, as the other Nazi struck the courier, the rope connecting the courier's aide snapped the aide into Marcel, forcing him to open his jaws. The second German staggered away and immediately drew his Luger. Quickly, he pumped two shots into the aide, two into the other Nazi, two into the courier, and two into the man who had just left the stall. The man staggered to the door, bleeding heavily from the elbows. "I think I'm canceling my subscription," he muttered.

The German nearest the courier grabbed for the briefcase just as Paul lunged to stop him. The German slammed the toilet seat down on Paul's hand. "Ze case is chained to ze courier's wrist!" he yelled to his companion.

"Shoot ze lock off it, zen," said the other Nazi, holding his Luger on Marcel, "and remove ze papers. Are you seriously wounded?"

"No, ze bullets are in my stomach. By tomorrow I'll haf zem digested."

There was another shot, and then the two Germans ran from the room, the one from the stall holding the papers. Paul and Marcel helped up the courier and the courier's aide, and the four of them staggered back into the club. Ahead, they could see the Germans returning to Schlissel's table. The Frenchmen rejoined Marlene.

"What happened?" she asked.

"Don't ask," said Paul.

"But . . . there were shots."

"A car backfiring."

"Eight times?"

Paul sighed. "There was a fight. The Germans jumped us and took the documents."

"But . . . there were only two of them. There are four of you."

"*Oui*. But two of us were roped together. Also, they are untrained in French foot-fighting, which gives them a tremendous advantage." He put his right hand inside the left flap of his coat.

"Tell me," said Marlene, "do you think of yourself as a famous short French dictator?"

"Wha?"

"Your hand . . ."

"Oh." Paul shrugged. "They slammed the seat down on it. I'm all right."

"But the gunshots? I thought you were—"

"No, *madame*," gasped the courier, bleeding from the nose. "It was us."

The courier's head and the aide's head struck the table simultaneously as they collapsed.

"Are they—?" asked Marlene.

"What?" said Paul.

"Covered for this sort of injury."

Paul examined the courier and then the aide. "The

courier has been shot in the nose," he announced. "Apparently, he's had an allergic reaction to the bullet and has died. The aide is also dead, having been shot in the rope."

"The rope?"

"It snapped his waist. I don't know how he even made it out here."

"I'll take care of this," said Marcel. He turned and clapped his hands. "Busboy! Clean off this table, please."

Marlene looked distraught. "Without the papers, we are prisoners here. We are. . . . "

"Screwed," said Paul.

"Yes. Screwed. What will we do, Paul?"

Paul grew pensive. "I don't know, my dear. Perhaps . . . open a nursing home."

Just then, Lou and Betty passed their table.

"Sorry about Paris, folks," said Lou.

Marcel looked after him. "It may just be that there *is* one man in San Francisco who can help us," he said thoughtfully. And then, after a moment, "Or maybe not."

Lou unlocked the door of his apartment, and he and Betty went in. He was desperately fatigued, tired to the point of passing out.

"Why don't you make yourself a drink?" he said to Betty. "I've just gotta catch some shut-eye. Wake me in about twenty minutes and we'll get acquainted."

He fell heavily on the bed. Betty crawled in after him. "Freddie? Oh, Freddie? Come on, Freddie, Betty's got something nice for you. Fred?" She lay on top of him and kissed the back of his neck, but he didn't move. "Fred?"

He was out cold.

She punched him on the back, and still he didn't

stir. "Oh Fred, don't be a creep. Please don't turn out to be a creep."

She got up and walked into the tiny kitchen. Two boxes of crackers lay on the table; half a dozen dishes were in the sink. The refrigerator held a jar of peanut butter, some near-rancid milk, two stalks of celery, and a small microscope. She walked back into the living room area just in time to see the door push open and a filthy, repulsive, limping old salt enter the apartment.

"Who—"

Hoppy put his hand over his lips. "An old friend," he said. "It's a surprise visit."

Betty moved toward the bed alcove.

"No, no," said Hoppy. "Let him sleep. He needs his sleep." He walked over to a chair and sat down. "I'm no problem. I'm here to help him. Soon's I rest m'knee, I'm gonna fix up a bit. If I know Lou, he hasn't washed his clothes in six months."

"You don't exactly look like a cleanliness champion, either," said Betty.

"Don't judge by appearances," said Hoppy. "Say, can I make ya some coffee?"

Betty nodded, and Hoppy got up and went into the kitchen. "Used to work for Mr. Peckinpaugh," he called from inside. "Last assignment, he blew me up, which is why I'm a bit slow in recoverin'. Say, you wouldn't have any extra string on yuh, would you, ma'am? Can't seem to find any here."

"Sorry," said Betty, relaxing finally now that she saw the old man was harmless. Men, she thought. Look how they live. If the world were left to them, we'd be back in medieval times. Smallpox and plague. Vassals and serfs. Knights in armor having their way with any woman they wanted.

After a moment, Hoppy brought out the coffee,

placed it on the cocktail table, and sat down next to her on the couch.

"Sometimes," said Betty, "I wish I were back in the Middle Ages."

"Oh, me too, ma'am," said Hoppy, scratching under his arms. "When I was forty or forty-five, I had all m' juices then." He leaned over and whispered. "I could take on five women in a row, and satisfy 'em all. Or one woman five times, if she wanted it."

Betty smiled. "Brag, brag. I haven't yet met a man who wasn't finished for the night after one little pop." She looked at the bed. "Some are finished after no pops."

Hoppy placed down his coffee. His hands were quivering. "I . . . I could show ya a little something."

"Never mind."

"Course, I ain't in m' Middle Ages no more, but ole Hoppy still got a few juices left."

Betty shook her head. "Sorry, I don't go for sailors."

Hoppy began to plead. "Oh, please, mum, just offer ole Hoppy a little tidbit. It's been so long since I got anything at all. Last I had was eight years ago in Montana, an' that was a sheep. Beautiful sheep she was, too, with beautiful curly hair. But nothin' at all since, an' ole Hop is dyin' fer it."

"I'm waiting for Fred," said Betty.

"It don't have to be much, mum," said Hoppy. "Hop's got a terrific imagination. I'm imaginin' right now I got a knee, fer example. Please—fer a friend of Mr. Peckinpaugh's?"

Betty sipped her coffee, then put down the cup. "Tell you what, you can't touch, but I'll give you a glimpse."

"Oh, God," said Hoppy, clasping his hands together. "Oh God, m' prayers are answered." He ducked down behind the couch.

100

"Where are you going?"

"I'm just gonna do some things to myself while you give me that peek. They're somewhat disgustin', ma'am, and involve me playin' with m' lower echelons. You needn't worry none, though."

Betty positioned herself sideways on the couch as Hoppy crouched down beside one armrest. Slowly, she hiked up her skirt. His eyes widened. Violent thrashings and convulsions engulfed him, and then, suddenly, he was still.

"That was one of the most perverted, degenerate things I've ever been involved with," said Betty.

"Thank you," said Hoppy.

"I'm going in to Fred now," said Betty. "We're going to play a game."

But Hoppy had passed out. Betty got up and walked over to the bed. Lou was snoring. She quickly unzipped her dress, removed her bra, panties, and high-heeled shoes, and lay down on top of him.

"Mmm," said Lou.

Betty began to move. "Come on, Fred, you've had your rest."

"Mmm."

"Come on. Big mama's here and I've got something wet, warm, and wonderful for you."

Lou snapped awake. "Oatmeal?" he said.

"Better," said Betty.

He rolled over, but she still stayed on top of him. "Are you protected against unwanted pregnancies?" he asked.

"Yes," she said, kissing his eyes, nose, lips, and neck and undoing the buttons of his shirt. "I'm protected by abstention. It's over ninety percent effective." She helped him lower his pants.

"I really should be getting some sleep," said Lou. She removed his underpants and ran her fingers gently over his groin. "You've got a beautiful set of ulterior motives," she said.

"I hope they're in working condition," said Lou.

"The initial indications are favorable," said Betty, lowering herself onto him. She moaned. "Oh God, are they favorable!"

A ringing. The sound came crashing into Lou's brain. He stretched out a hand. Rrrrrrring! He fumbled for the alarm clock. Rrrrrring! He propped himself up and focused his eyes. Eight-fifteen. Eight-fifteen in the morning.

And suddenly, the ringing stopped.

"It's your nickel."

Lou looked up and saw Betty. She had answered the phone and was standing by the side of his bed, smoking a cigarette. She was also wearing his robe, which had dozens of laundry tags attached all over it.

"Who wants to speak to him?" said Betty. She listened for a response.

"All right, all right. Just a minute." She handed the phone to Lou. "Wouldn't say who he was."

Lou took the receiver, and motioned to Betty to give him her cigarette.

"Yeah," he said into the mouthpiece.

"Mr. Peckinpaugh?" came the voice.

"Yeah."

"I believe you had the distinct pleasure of meeting Mr. Damascus last night."

"That's right," said Lou. "He distincted the place up. Who is this?"

"Jasper Blubber."

"Blubber, eh? Yeah, he mentioned you."

Lou opened a side drawer and removed a glass of freshly squeezed orange juice. He drank it down.

102

"Would it be possible to meet you today?" said Blubber.

"It's possible," said Lou. "Lots of things are possible. Man may someday go to the moon, though I'd doubt it. Women may someday take a pill to prevent pregnancy, though I'd doubt it. There might even be an expressway that would go from Manhattan to the far end of Long Island, although now we're entering the realm of fantasy."

"I am interested," said Blubber, "in discussing the 'missing item,' shall we say, so to speak, if you will."

"Ah, yes. The item."

"Then you would be, perhaps, conceivably available?"

"Sure. Why not, by your leave, as it were."

"Splendid!" said Blubber. "I like a man who doesn't mince words."

"I don't slice carrots, either," said Lou.

"Twelve noon," said Blubber. "At the bar of the Crusades Hotel."

"How will I recognize you?"

Blubber chuckled. "You'll have no trouble there, sir. I'm an extra large man."

"Must be tough to find trousers."

"I'll be sitting on the first two stools as you come in."

The phone clicked off, and Lou hung up. He rose from the bed and put on a robe that had been slung over the edge of the dresser. Then he walked into the living area, where he found a full breakfast for two laid out on the table. A long-stemmed rose sat in a thin vase filled with water.

"Betty," he said, "that is really beautiful."

"I agree," she said.

"Well, where did you get the rose from?"

"Oh, I didn't get it," said Betty sweetly. "And I didn't make breakfast, either."

103

Just then, Hoppy came limping out of the kitchen. He held a steaming pot of coffee.

"Mornin', Lou. Sleep good?"

He grinned and made a low growling sound in his throat. Then he poured the coffee into two cups. Lou just stared.

"How long has *he* been here?" he asked grouchily.

Betty bit into a piece of toast and then took a forkful of eggs-and-onions. "All night."

"Huh?"

"Sat right there on the couch."

"You mean while we were—"

Betty nodded.

"That's disgraceful," said Lou, "to do that to an old man. Just because he's old doesn't mean he's lost his faculties."

"Still got m' faculties," agreed Hoppy, "although they're gettin' a mite shriveled."

"I told him we were playing doctor," said Betty.

"Did he buy it?"

"Beats me."

"Naw," said Hoppy, chuckling. "I knowed you was fuckin'. You think ole Hop don' know 'bout such activities? Ole Hop damn near invented 'em."

"And of course you stayed to watch," said Lou.

"I told you I'd watch after you, Lou," said Hoppy. "Never knew bodyguardin' could be such fun."

He limped back into the kitchen then with his special, syncopated, *chambo* rhythm. There was a knock on the door.

"Who's there?" said Lou.

"Eet is the Western Union."

"Come on, don't hand me that."

"All right, it is Marcel from the club."

"Are you alone?"

"No," said a second voice. "I am with Marcel from the club."

104

"And who're you?" asked Lou.

"I am Paul DuChard, the hero."

"What do you want?"

Marcel answered. "A chance to make the world a pure, sweet, safe place wtih a balanced harmony among all nature's creatures so that children can sing in the streets once more."

"I'm not sure how much of this I can take," said Lou, but he unlocked the door and opened it. Marcel and DuChard entered quickly.

"I'm sorry," said Marcel, looking around, "I thought you were alone."

Hoppy came out of the kitchen. "They don't care," he said, indicating Betty and Lou. "They even let me watch 'em makin' mookie-oonoo."

"It's okay," said Lou. "The girl can be trusted. She'll keep her mouth shut."

"She didn't last night," volunteered Hoppy.

"It's the old man I worry about," said Marcel. "Can we talk in front of him?"

"Talk?" said Lou. "What about what we did?" He sat down on the bed, and Betty leaned on him playfully. "All right, what can I do for you boys?"

"*Monsieur* Peckinpaugh," said Paul, "last night certain documents belonging to me were stolen."

"You're sure they're stolen?" interrupted Lou. "You haven't just misplaced them? It's a common thing. A great number of my clients who report things stolen later come back and have—"

"A toilet seat was slammed on my hand!" said Paul. "An innocent man was prevented from reading his newspaper! Yes, they were stolen. Robbed from me before my eyes."

"And mine," said Marcel.

"Okay," said Lou. "Just checking."

"I need your help in recovering the papers," said Paul.

Lou tilted his head. "You can pay, of course."

"We are not wealthy people, *monsieur*. We lost over two million francs in zee stock market," said Paul.

"That's a lot of dough."

"Yes. We invested heavily in a company that claimed to have found a cure for baldness using a substance derived from manure."

"Seems farfetched."

"For eight weeks in a row, they covered the heads of fifty volunteers with shit. There was much promise."

"But, of course, nothing came up," said Lou.

"Ah, *non,* very much came up," said Marcel. "Except, it was not hair, it was grass. Rye grass. By summer, these men had a 'lush carpet of verdant green,' as the advertisements said. Eeet was terrible. They had to mow their heads once a week. Many of them had weeds, which had to be painfully extracted. Some were attacked by chinchbugs. All in all, a disaster. Zee company, of course, went bankrupt."

"And then," said Paul, "we went ahead and bet on zee war. Over four million francs before we knew what happened."

"Who'd you have?" asked Lou.

"We took France, of course," said Paul, "at eight to five."

"They suckered you."

Paul removed a pocket watch with much ornate metalwork evident on the case. "I have a gold watch, *monsieur,* that was given to me by the President of the Republic."

"I already got a watch," said Lou.

"Yes, but this one is very valuable," said Paul. "And it plays a lovely little tune. It's yours if you will help us."

He handed the watch to Lou, who opened it and

106

put it next to his ear. He heard a voice. "President Roosevelt announced today that in view of the recent upturn in the economy, funds for the Civilian Conservation Corps are to be cut back—"

"What the hell is this?" said Lou.

"You must have the news," said Paul. "Rotate zee entire case counterclockwise and you get zee tune."

Lou did as instructed, and presently, he heard a voice that was unmistakably Maurice Chevalier's. There was a full orchestral accompaniment. "Mimi, you funny little, sunny little, Mimi, are you the one . . . ?" Lou closed the watch, and the music stopped abruptly. He handed it back to Paul.

"I never cared for him. I don't find him charming. He lays on me like a piece of rotten fish."

"I am sorry, *monsieur*," said Paul.

"Do you have anything in a rhumba, maybe? Or even a samba?"

Paul shook his head no.

"Too bad," said Lou, "but this ain't a pawnshop. I'm walking around with rented bullets for my gun."

"But this is a matter of national concern," said Paul. "The honor of France is involved."

"We all got problems," said Lou.

"Perhaps," said Paul, "when America is confronted by war you'll think differently."

"When the wolves are nipping your boots," said Marcel, "and the salamanders are crawling on your tibia, your tone will change. But then, it will be too late."

Lou shrugged.

Paul motioned to Marcel, and they both moved out into the hallway. "Thank God, I think as a Frenchman," he said. *"Vive la France!"*

"Vive la République," said Marcel.

"Hooray for Hollywood," said Lou, closing the door.

"Vive la différence," said Betty, coming up behind Lou and massaging his neck. "I like the way you handled yourself, Fred."

"I do all right."

"Course it wasn't as good as the way your friend Hoppy handled himself last night."

Hoppy wagged his head from side to side. "When you lifted your skirt, mum, ole Hop thought he were about to die. Ole Hop hasn't been so excited since he seen a girdle ad in *Life* magazine. But last night was like an oasis in the desert, an' old Hop rub his magic lamp so hard he thought a genie would appear. You done a wonderful, charitable act, mum, an' I believe it be tax deductible, too."

"That was very nice of you," said Lou.

"I felt sorry for the old coot," said Betty. "It was either that, or go out and buy him string."

Lou walked over to the bureau and removed an envelope from the top.

"Here, take this," he said, handing it to Betty. "And if you thank me, so help you, I'll slug you."

"What is it?"

"A ticket."

"To where?"

"Africa. A girl like you with a voice like yours has no place singing in a dump like America."

He went back into the bed alcove then, and nonchalantly began getting dressed. Betty followed.

"Can't take it, can you, Fred?"

Lou ignored her.

"Can't take it when someone like me gets too close, huh?"

"Listen," said Lou, "a friend of mine owns a little club on the Ivory Coast. He's a good Joe, but he's got a touch of leprosy. I don't like to open his letters and, in person, I'd be leery about shaking his hand. I'll see you around, Slinky."

108

He walked to the door, opened it, and handed her her coat.

"Is that it?" she said.

Lou looked around. "Is what it? You missing something?"

"Yeah, I'm missing something," said Betty. "I mean, is this the way it ends? I walk to the door, you hand me my coat and say, 'See you around, Slinky.'"

Lou looked puzzled. He scratched his head. "Listen, uh, I'm a very literal type guy. I mean what am I supposed to do here? Throw you out the window? Ask you to marry me? Advise you on the latest bargains in rebuilt carburetors?"

Betty just stood there and shook her head. "There's no way I can explain it, Fred." She moved into the doorway. "I suppose that's the way it goes. But if you ever get lonely, Fred. . . ."

"Yeah."

"Just call me. You know how to dial, don't you? Just put your finger in the little round hole—"

"Oh, Hop's gettin' excited again, mum," said Hoppy, who'd wandered over.

"Get her out of here!" said Lou, pushing Betty into the hall.

Hoppy followed. "I'll go with her for a while," he said. "Maybe one day she'll get desperate and there'll be no one around and she might let an old salt get into her wound."

"Dream," said Betty.

But the door had closed.

Inside, the phone rang for the fourth time.

"Hello?" said Lou, when he'd finally reached it.

"Mr. Peckinpaugh?"

The voice was high and whiny and smelled of vinegar mixed with rear-end lubricant.

"Yes," said Lou.

"This is Pepe Damascus. I can't talk to you now."

The phone clicked dead. Nice of him to tell me that, thought Lou. Always good to have a client who keeps me informed. He finished dressing and carefully combed his hair. He was about to go to a most interesting meeting.

VII

Betty studied the ticket. It was for a Japanese steamer, the *Hibachi Maru,* bound for the Ivory Coast by way of the Camay Republic, the Dove Islands, and the United Palmolive Emirates.

"Take us about six months sailing time," said Hoppy.

"Whaddaya mean, 'us'?"

"Us means we two. I'm going along."

"You don't have a ticket."

"Oh, ole Hop find work. He knows ships better'n anyone. Ole Hop swab the deck, clean out the hold, scrape barnacles, get blind and deaf in the engine room. He a useful character. Everybody love."

"Well, not me," said Betty.

Downstairs, she waved for a cab to take her back to her apartment.

"I can give you some small pleasures, mum," Hoppy persisted. "Six months at sea is a long time for a woman of strong appetites. Long time even for someone who don't eat nothin'."

A taxi pulled over, and Betty got in.

"Hop is awful good at lickin' a woman's toes," yelled the old man after the departing cab. "Hop's tongue so wonderful, he can even get under the nails." He stood alone in the street. "Hop give great callous and bunion jobs." he said forlornly.

In the apartment, Betty packed quickly. There wasn't all that much to take. Three or four show costumes, some underwear, shoes, a thirteen-volume dictionary, toilet articles, a map of Antarctica, her ant collection, a few two-by-fours, and six cans of sardines. On the way to the waterfront, she stopped off at the library and took out a book by a young Ivory Coast writer, a fantasy entitled *I Ate the Prime Minister for Dinner*. It was late in the afternoon when she arrived at the pier from which the Hibachi Maru was scheduled to depart.

She showed her tickets at the window.

"Ah, yes, very good," said the young Japanese man through the grating. "This entitle bearer to one free ride to Ivory Coast, cargo class."

"Cargo class?" said Betty. "What the hell is that?"

"Ah," said the man smiling politely. "Is nothing to be ashame. Oh, no. I myself have many relatives came to this country that way."

"Oh," said Betty., "Thank God. I was beginning to think—"

"Visit them often in cemetery," said the man. "Burn much incense in their memories."

"All right," said Betty. "What is cargo class?"

"Just what it say," explained the man, still smiling. "You treated with same politeness we reserve for wheat, rice, bamboo shoots, and raw fish. In fact, you

112

share compartment with these commodities. True, you not entitle to ruxury of steerage class passenger, but you get to destination same as them."

"Terrific," said Betty.

"You have ruggage?"

"Yes." Betty placed her luggage on a small platform.

"You have all papers?"

"What papers?"

"What you think?" said the man, grinning. "*News* and *Mirror*? Hee-hee. I make rittle joke. No, I mean passport, visa, stuff rike that."

Betty looked stunned. "Oh my God, I completely forgot!" She held her head. "It just totally escaped me. Oh, God, now I can't get out of the U.S.A."

"Oh, you get out," said the man. "You just can't come back in. Also, you need inocuration."

"What?"

"Shot. Injection." He pantomined a needle being jabbed into his arm. "Must get smallpox, yes? Typhoid. Malaria. Beriberi, agar-agar, pellagra, and scurvy. American susceptible all disease, catch everything."

Betty grabbed up her luggage. "All right. You got me. I am an idiot."

"Not your fault," said the man. "All Occidental the same. Have IQ of *nunchako* stick."

Betty began walking away. "I couldn't have gone anyway," she said. "The fine on my overdue library book would've made me a pauper for life."

The cab pulled up in front of the Crusades Hotel, and Lou got out almost before it came to a halt. He paid the driver and approached the front entrance. The hotel's architecture was patterned after the Eastern Byzantine style of King Cyrus III, a madman who crucified ten thousand barbers after getting a haircut

113

that took a little too much off the top. The style was characterized by the so-called "sitting buttress" and an expansive liver-and-onions motif carved into the decorative stonework. Lou entered without looking up.

On the right, in the lobby, he saw a sign that said "The St. John The Divine Bar." There was an arrow, and he followed it to a curtained archway beyond which sat a man reading a newspaper. The man's face was hidden, but to the trained eye . . . there were signs.

Lou passed and lit a cigarette. "Hi ya, kid. No school today?"

The man put the paper down. It was the Follower, wearing the same hat he'd worn that day he'd tailed Lou, and the same floor-length overcoat. He looked balefully at Lou.

"You better watch it, Mac."

"Or?"

"Or you're gonna be pickin' up your teeth wit' two broken arms."

"Ah," said Lou. "Very good. You learn that from your little friends on the street?"

The Follower extended his index finger. "Keep ridin' me, Mac. You go ahead. Keep it up."

"And? There's always an 'and.' "

"And they'll bury you in forty-two different cemeteries."

Lou knew he'd have to keep vigilant until this case was over. Punks like this were not dangerous when you could see them, but anyone from the shadows—from an alley, in a darkened hallway at night—anyone could kill anyone else. And this kid was definitely bonkers.

"Cranky, aren't you?" said Lou.

The Follower stiffened with rage.

"It always happens when your second teeth start

114

coming in." Lou entered the curtained archway without looking back.

He saw him almost immediately, sitting on a stool near the end of the semicircular bar. A well-dressed, enormous whale of a man, drinking from a huge mug of beer and munching on pretzels. Lou crossed the room and came up behind him.

"Blubber?"

The man turned to Lou, and there was fury in his face. Mean, pig eyes blazed from a mask of hardened fat. Surprised, Lou looked around, his eyes gradually accommodating to the dim light. His gaze swept the semicircle of the bar. Seated at it were six other men, all huge, none less than three hundred pounds. One of them said to him, sneering, "Who did you call 'Blubber'?"

"I can explain this," said Lou quickly.

"Go ahead," said another man. Two more got down off their stools.

"Blubber is the name of someone," said Lou nervously.

The remaining fat men stood up and began approaching him.

"Blubber is a term of endearment," said Lou. Looking around, bird-like, he began to back away, but one of the fat men moved with surprising quickness to cut off his path.

"Look, really, fellas, I'm not interested in any trouble."

At that point the Follower stuck his head in the door. "Kill 'im, boys! Crush his head, stamp his spinal cord, mash his balls, ravel his socks. Cause him mental anguish and loss of services."

"Thanks for putting in a word," said Lou.

"We gonna have to teach you a lesson," said the first fat man. "The lesson is, respect those heavier than yourself."

Lou had assumed the *Tae Kwon Do* karate fighting pose, front foot pointed forward, leg bent at the knee, rear leg also bent but foot pointing sideways. His front arm was vertical, his rear arm horizontal and covering his stomach, both hands balled into tight fists. "Look," he said, "I'm a master of martial arts, you guys are all big men. Someone's gonna get hurt. How about a truce?"

His antagonists had all assumed the fat man's fighting pose, cheeks puffed, stomach thrust aggressively forward, thighs rubbing together. "No truce," said one of the men.

"We got a club here," the first one explained, still advancing. "We call it Weight Gainers. We meet Tuesdays and Fridays."

"You mean this is a weight-reducing group?" asked Lou, circling cautiously to his left.

"A weight-augmenting group," said one of the men. "We've all tried to lose. It's too hard. Much easier to gain, so that's what we do. We each have goals and special diets; we come here and weigh in on meat scales."

"But it's bad for your health," said Lou.

"You mean it's bad for yours," said the first fat man, moving in and taking a ponderous swing at Lou's jaw.

The man obviously expected a sidestep, or some other evasive maneuver, but instead, Lou blocked the punch with his forearm and executed a *Yup Chagi* side kick to the abdomen. The man said, "Uh," but seemed unaffected.

"Jesus," said Lou.

A second man came up behind him and put his arm around Lou's neck. Quickly, Lou brought back his elbow in a vicious move, catching his opponent under the ribs. He was surprised when the man did not let go. Lou stamped down with his heel on the man's right foot and felt the grip loosen. Again. It loosened further, and he squirmed out. "What's a matter, haven't got enough fat on your toes?" he taunted. The man charged at him then, a rhinoceros in a made-to-order suit, and Lou was readying a simple *Chung-kwon Chigi* (to go) when suddenly his arms were pinned behind him. There was no time to react. He was a thin piece of salami between two huge rolls.

Briefly, he lost consciousness, rammed into oblivion by six hundred fifty pounds of fat on the run. The air was squeezed from his chest; his ribs collapsed like an umbrella. When the men rebounded, he reeled away, gasping for air, and, oxygen-drunk, staggered out the archway entrance.

"Hello," said the Follower, pleasantly. "Nice to see you here. I hope you're having a pleasant stay."

Lou did not bother to choke out a response. When a few moments had passed, and he got his breath, he straightened his tie and headed back.

"Trying another quick round?" said the Follower.

Lou lashed out and smacked him on the wrist. "Any more naughty comments, and Daddy's going to circumcise you with a pair of pliers. Now be a good boy—or girl, or whatever."

He pulled his hat down over his face and reentered. The fat men had re-seated themselves, and Lou cautiously pushed forward. I don't know why I'm doing this, he thought. They're just going to beat the piss out of me again. No amount of karate can overcome 2200 pounds of angry fat. Suddenly, he heard a voice.

"Over here, Mr. Peckinpaugh."

Lou turned and made out a booth near one wall, nearly invisible in the dim light. He approached and saw a man sprawling on one of the seats.

"I . . . am Jasper Blubber."

"Good," said Lou. "I was afraid I'd have to page you. They would have beat my brains in." He sat down.

Blubber was a mountainous creature, a walrus in business attire, a collection of fat cells run amok. His ankles dripped over the tops of his shoes; his cheeks sprawled below his jaw. Even his elbows were fat. He stirred the tall drink in front of him.

"You do drink, of course."

"Why not," said Lou.

Blubber snapped his fingers. "One Gin Sling!"

A waiter appeared.

"I'd rather have a brandy," said Lou.

"One Gin Sling is the waiter," said Blubber.

"Chinese or Korean?" said Lou, studying the man's features.

"Dutch," said the waiter.

"One brandy, One Gin Sling," said Blubber.

The waiter nodded and left.

Lou looked apprehensively at the bar. "They get a 'large' crowd here, don't they?"

"The word is 'hard-to-fit,'" said Blubber. "Or 'portly,' if you prefer."

"All right, portly."

"Yes," said Blubber. "I must be discreet in my business. This is the one place in town I'm not noticed."

"You're accustomed to being around portly people, then?"

"Yes," said Blubber, chuckling. "Been inside one all my life. Spent years trying to get out. Years. Joined this diet group, Slobs Anonymous, and took off sixty pounds once, but gained it back the next day."

"The next *day?*"

"Ate half a cow. I've tried everything. Every fad. Even had a staple put in my ear. Didn't lose any weight, just kept hearing the sounds of staplers.

Weight-loss books—you name 'em, I've read 'em. Last one was *Dr. Altman's Ex-Lax and Mortar Diet.* You shit bricks."

Lou grinned.

"But let me not waste your time, sir, and get down to business. What arrangements have you made with the woman?"

"Which woman?"

"The woman who came to your office. Natasha Ublenskaya."

Lou nodded philosophically. "Good. I thought you were talking about someone else. She wanted me to find my partner's murderer."

Blubber raised his head. "Ah, yes. Your esteemed associate, Mr. Merkrel."

"Merkle. Obviously, she and Damascus are after the same thing."

"Obviously."

"And so are you, unless I miss my guess."

The waiter returned to their table and placed Lou's drink in front of him.

"So you're Dutch, huh," said Lou.

"Dutch East Indies," said the man, bowing slightly. "Educated at Harvard, now taking masters in Oriental studies at UCLA."

"Very impressive," said Lou. "But why are you in Frisco working as a waiter?"

"Research for thesis," said the man, "entitle, the *Role of the Chinese Restaurant in Modern Society.*"

"Sounds very scholarly," said Lou. When the waiter left, he returned his attention to Blubber. "Was my guess correct about what you're after?"

"Your reputation is not unwarranted, sir," said Blubber. "Drink up and I'll tell you an astounding story."

Lou took a sip and quickly put the glass down. "This is a Gin Sling."

"It is?" said Blubber. "Then I was wrong. The waiter's name is Brandy."

"That would account for it," said Lou.

"Now," said Blubber, "in eighteen twenty-three, a little-known historical fact occurred. Twelve Albanian fishermen, armed only with fishhooks and penknives, conquered China, Tibet, and Mongolia. For nearly fifty years they ruled the world's largest land mass."

"That's remarkable," said Lou. "I never knew that."

"That's because you didn't take history in Albania."

"That's because I didn't take mythology, you mean," said Lou.

"No," said Blubber. "No myth. At least about the final facts. Eventually, the men returned home with the richest spoils of war—"

"Why do they call it spoils?" asked Lou. "I've always wondered about that. "Why don't they ever come home with the good stuff, why only the spoils?"

"Ah, but they did come home with the good stuff," said Blubber. "The best ever documented. Each man had a seven-hundred-sixty-carat diamond, the size and shape of a large brown double-A New Jersey egg."

"A New Jersey, huh," marveled Lou.

"Each diamond egg is worth in excess of a quarter-million dollars."

"You don't say?" said Lou. He whistled through his teeth.

"I do, sir. I just did. I said it, ask anyone."

"I believe you, although it's hard. I mean that's more than twice the price of a regular egg. Go on."

"Eventually the diamond eggs became the property of the Albanian government. Some years later they were stolen, along with some chickens, by a band of Polish gypsies."

"Here goes," said Lou.

"Here goes what?"

"You're gonna tell me now that the gypsies ate the eggs, right?"

"No," said Blubber, "but they spent three years trying to crack them."

"Is that so?"

"It is," said Blubber, "I swear it on the medals of my grandfather."

"This is sacred to you?"

"They were for growing vegetables. Two years in a row, he grew the largest cucumber in his village. We were all very proud of him. I swear it. I have photographs showing me swearing to it."

"I believe you," said Lou. "Go on."

"They last showed up in Paris in nineteen twenty-one."

"Who didn't?"

"A clever designer had strung all twelve eggs together and sold it as a necklace to a wealthy woman."

"She must've been a weight-lifter."

"She was trying to conceal a double chin," said Blubber. "The woman was murdered, sir, and it disappeared."

"The double chin?"

"The necklace of eggs. I don't know what became of the chin."

"End of story?" said Lou.

Blubber chuckled patronizingly. "The beginning for me. I made an exhaustive search of police records and traveled half the world interviewing people. I spread a great deal of money around and used a good deal of influence, and I finally came up with the name of the murderer." There was a pregnant pause.

"All right," said Lou. I'll bite. Is it someone famous?"

"No."

"Is it a woman?"

"No."

"Is he or she human?"

"His name is Vladimir Tserijemiwtz, and he was a Rumanian sailor. Seems he lost a great deal of money speculating in snails and got himself heavily in debt. His creditors kept tightening the strings, and one day they told him that unless he paid up immediately, he'd wind up at the bottom of the Black Sea wearing wooden shoes."

"You mean cement shoes."

"His creditors were Polish lumber magnates. At any rate, the threat apparently frightened him enough to cause him to commit murder."

Lou nodded. "What was his name again?"

Blubber shook his head. "I was afraid you'd ask that. I can't say it without spitting."

Lou ducked sideways.

"Vladimir Tserijemiwtz."

Lou raised his head cautiously. "But if this . . . Vladimir stole the diamonds eggs to pay off his creditors, then what's your interest in him? You should be tracing the creditors."

Blubber grinned. "Correct . . . except he never did pay. Apparently, the size of his new fortune exceeded anything he'd ever expected."

"So he ran away, is that it? And you're looking for him?"

"Sixteen years, I've spent," said Blubber. "Sixteen years and every penny I have, tracking down this man. And at last I've found him."

"You mean you've—"

"From Rumania, he made his way overland to Bulgaria, dyeing his hair in the meantime, and growing a mustache. He stayed in Bulgaria for eight months, working in a mop factory until he could get enough cash to obtain a forged passport and make his way to Turkey. In Turkey, he shaved his head completely and grew a beard. He was there two years, carving toilet seats, until he caught a steamer for Norway. In Norway, he let his hair grow back and dyed it blond and changed his name to Sven Lündgren. Three years later, posing as a reindeer trainer, he got a flight to Johannesburg, South Africa, where he dyed his skin and hair black and—"

"Can you shorten this up a bit?" said Lou.

"He worked in the gold mines as a laborer for seven years, twelve hours a day underground, one day a week rest. At this point, the Polish creditors finally gave up looking for him."

"I wonder why," said Lou.

"The day came when Vladimir migrated to the U.S., coming here by way of Argentina, of course, then Paraguay, Cuba, and Mexico City."

"The usual route."

"He entered as a Mexican, quickly cut his hair short and dyed it blond again, and removed his beard and mustache and assumed the identity of a Tucson engineering executive."

"He had since removed the black skin dye he used as a South African miner?"

"No, not removed it. Covered it. With a white skin dye. He stayed in Tucson for a year, then moved to Denver where—"

"I can't take much more," said Lou.

"You?" bellowed Blubber. "What about me? I had to track down all this shit. Anyway, in Denver he sold tee-shirts with one long sleeve, one short, and finally—and this is the point—moved to San Francisco."

Lou sat up. "You mean—?"

"Yes. Precisely. Right now, he is here in San Francisco, as surely as you're sitting there drinking the wrong drink." He snapped his fingers. "Waiter!"

A new waiter approached.

"Another round here," said Blubber.

The man nodded.

"Wait a minute," said Lou. "Where's the other waiter?"

"Off duty," said the man.

"What's your name?"

"Daiquiri."

"Never mind," said Lou. "I'll just have coffee." The waiter nodded, and left.

"You were saying. . . ." said Lou to Blubber.

"The diamonds are almost in my grasp," said the fat man. "Vladimir Tserijemiwtz is living in splendor somewhere in the city. He has changed his name by making an anagram of his original name." He removed a piece of paper from his pocket.

"This is gonna be fun," said Lou. "Did you know that the letters of my last name, when rearranged, spell 'Pee in pack, ugh'?"

"They do? That's remarkable."

"Well, you have to add an extra 'e,' " said Lou. "But it's legit except for that."

"I have been trying to unscramble this one," said Blubber, "for over seven years to no avail."

"Can I see that?" said Lou.

Blubber handed him the sheet of paper. "Don't waste your time, sir. I've had well-paid experts give up on it."

Lou studied the sheet. On the top of the page was written VLADIMIR TSERIJEMIWTZ, and beneath, a columnar listing of names:

VADIRIML TIJEWTZMISER
LIVADIMR JEMITERISWTZ
MALIVIRD ZTWIMESTEVIR
SEYMOUR K. SCHWARTZ
MARY TYLER MALAMAR
etc.

"Some of these are not at all obvious," said Lou. "As I said, experts worked for years, Mr. Pee-in-pack . . . uh, Peckinpaugh. Now—once I find him, the rest is academic. Blackmail, pure and simple. Either he hands over the diamonds to me or I hand him over to the authorities."

"On what charge?"

Blubber chuckled. "Obeseticide."

"Obeseticide?"

"The murdering of a fat woman."

Lou nodded. "Mind if I keep this list?"

"Not at all," said Blubber.

The Follower came in and approached their table.

"Friend of yours?" said Lou.

"He works for me, yes," acknowledged Blubber. "Friend, no. He tried to rape an evergreen bush in front of my hotel."

The Follower stooped and whispered something in Blubber's ear. Blubber nodded, and the Follower walked away, making an obscene gesture at Lou.

"Nice boy," said Lou.

"Background will show," said Blubber. "At any rate, I'm afraid our meeting has come to an end."

"Pity," said Lou. "I was enjoying it."

"We should leave separately," said Blubber. "It makes more sense for me to go first."

"Why is that?" asked Lou.

"Then I don't get stuck with the check."

"But what about our . . . business arrangement?"

"Consider us partners, Mr. Peckinpaugh. I'll contact you through the boy. Adieu, sir."

Blubber attempted to get up, but was unable to rise. He tried again, but his immense, overhanging stomach struck the table.

"Damnable low seats," he said. "Help me up, Mr. Peckinpaugh, will you please?"

Lou's lips stretched in a thin smile. He sprang to his feet. "That's what you got the kid for. If he has any time in between evergreen assaults, that is." He motioned to the bartender. "Drinks for everybody, compliments of the man stuck in the booth."

As he left, Lou tipped his hat to Blubber with great ceremony.

VIII

In the taxi going back, Lou tried to review the case in his mind, to list the salient facts and see if he could make some overall sense of them. One: his partner is shot and killed in a cheap hotel. Two: his partner's wife tries to shift the blame onto him, though they'd been lovers for nine years. Three: A crazy woman meets him at his office, pukes on his coat, and asks him to find her niece, supposedly the same job his partner had been on. Four: a man with a stinking voice meets him in a chic waterfront dive and informs him that the "niece" is really a valuable object and offers to split the proceeds if you will help him locate it. Five: at this same café he meets a woman who once threw him over, something Lou did not like since it bruised his buttocks and injured his pride. Six: the husband of the powerful woman appeals to him the next day to recover certain stolen documents. Seven: an immense tub of lard, referred to as "dangerous" by the stinking greaseball, sees him in a bar and identifies the valuable object as a diamond-egg necklace and its owner as someone now living in San Francisco. The tub also wants to be partners with Lou.

Lou directed the driver to pull over. "But why?" asked the cabbie. "Was it something I did? Something I said? A look, perhaps. A nuance?"

"I have a problem," said Lou, "and I've got to think about it." He gave the man a small tip.

"I'll never forget you, sir," said the driver. "The man who had me pull over for no reason, and then left a small but heartfelt tip. May God——"

"Never mind," said Lou, walking away.

"May God pee on you, sir!" yelled the driver suddenly as he rode off.

Lou walked along the street, turning the facts over and over and then under and under. Where was the pattern to it, the strand of reason, the telltale, linear progression of cause and effect? He came to a barber shop he recognized and stepped inside. He walked over to a man near the door. "Gino in today?"

The man looked around. "Gino in, but he busy. You wanna haircut, I give you."

Lou looked down the length of the shop. "How long a wait for Gino?"

The man hesitated. "Five hour."

"But there's no one here. The place is empty."

"All right," said the man. "You right. Four hour."

"Where is he?" said Lou. "I wanna see him."

The man hesitated. "I—I get."

Lou sat in a chair. After five minutes, Gino emerged through a rear curtain. He was a short, stocky Italian in his early fifties. He had thinning hair and wore rimless spectacles.

"Hey, Mr. Lou. Hey, how you been?"

"Not bad," said Lou. "Had a tough time getting past your man up front, though. Where is he, by the way?"

Gino motioned Lou over to a chair and flung a white sheet over him as he sat down. "Oh, you no mind him," he said. "He a new man. He right off boat. Thinks an hour is a minute."

Lou nodded. "All right, Gino, same as always. A little off the sides, a little off the back. Not too short."

Gino nodded and began working with the scissors. "One of these days, Mr. Lou, you gonna take off that hat. Then I be able to do your top."

"Not likely, Gino," said Lou. "Hey, Gino, what would you make of this?"

Quickly, Lou reviewed the facts of the case. He finished by describing Blubber and the diamond eggs. Gino, after ten minutes of snipping and cutting, gave Lou a fast shave and then removed the sheet. "I'd say you gotta two separate cases here," said Gino. "An' they gotta nothin' to do with each other. All you gotta do is find which facts go with which case, an' you in business."

Lou nodded thoughtfully. "You know, I think you got something."

"That's nine dollars," said Gino, ringing up the register.

"What?"

"Two for the consultation, seven for the haircut."

"Seven dollars for a haircut."

"A stylin'," said Gino. "I give you a stylin'.

Grumbling, Lou paid. On his way out, he saw the first barber emerge from the back and put on a coat.

"I quit," said the man. "I just realize. He say he pay me fifty cents an hour. I thought this means fifty a minute. I could do better in my original profession."

129

"What's that?" said Lou, as the two of them walked out the door.

"Dentist to animals," said the man. "Once I did root canal work on Lassie."

Lou entered his office and briskly closed the door behind him. Bess, seated at her desk, looked up and immediately put a finger over her lips, signaling that Lou should remain quiet. Bess had been his secretary for seventeen years and knew his every move, if not his every thought. She had brownish blond hair and wore frilly, feminine outfits and had been in love with her boss almost as long as she could remember. She spoke into the mouthpiece of the phone. "Yes, Mrs. Merkle. Yes. I know you did. Wait just a minute. Mr. Peck—?"

Lou shook his head no.

"No, he hasn't come in yet, Mrs. Merkle," continued Bess. She covered the phone with her hand and whispered to Lou. "You have a visitor in there. A Mrs. Sophia DeVega."

"What?" said the Widow Merkle, over the phone.

"I was just mumbling," said Bess, uncovering the mouthpiece.

"Pretty?" said Lou.

"Prettier than me, but I'm easier."

"I'm saving you for a rainy season," said Lou.

"Is he there with you?" screeched Mrs. Merkle over the phone. "You tell the truth now, is he there?"

"No, ma'am," said Bess. "We have a floor waxer in today."

Lou removed a piece of paper from his pocket. "You're good at crosswords. Try your hand at anagrams. See if you can come up with a name that makes sense out of this."

"And if I do?" said Bess.

"Do what?" said Mrs. Merkle. "No, I'm not complaining. You're entitled to have a floor waxer."

"If you can find it in the Frisco phone book," said Lou, "your rainy season may be tonight."

He opened the door to his office. "Mrs. DeVega, I presume."

The woman, seated in a chair, turned suddenly. She had platinum blond hair, and the smoke from her cigarette wound a coil above her head. There was . . . a curious air of familiarity about her, a sense not only of *déjà vu* but *plus-que-parfait*.

"Mr. Peckinpaugh?"

Lou's jaw dropped.

"You look startled."

"No, no," said Lou. "It's just that you look like fourteen other dames that was in here the other night."

The woman smiled with exaggerated shyness. "Yes, I know."

"You know?"

"Yes. They were my sister."

Lou nodded. "That explains the resemblance."

"Not to me," said the woman. "She was adopted."

"Yeah, well," seaid Lou, "so was I, but I don't look like your sister, either." He sat down behind his desk.

"Actually, you do resemble her a little," said the woman. "Your necks are similar."

"What can I do for you . . . Mrs. DeVega?"

"I want you to find someone for me."

"A date?" quipped Lou.

"I'm quite serious," said the woman.

"Sorry."

"I'm looking for my—for my—" The woman turned her head away and seemed to convulse. For the life of him, Lou could not tell whether she was laughing or crying.

"I'm sorry," she said finally. "I'm looking for— It's so hard for me to say it."

"For your echinococcus?" said Lou.

131

"No, no——"

"For your carpogonium?"

She took a deep breath and seemed to compose herself. "I would like for you to find my . . . husband and father."

"Two for the price of one?"

"They are the same man, Mr. Peckinpaugh."

Lou thought that over. "That would make you your own mother, wouldn't it?"

"I suppose, in some sense——"

"Is what you mean," said Lou slowly, "that you married your own father?"

"It's not like you think."

"I'm not making any judgments."

"It was a simple wedding," said the woman, "done very tastefully. There was no Viennese table at the end. The smorgasbord had only four hot dishes."

"I'm sure," said Lou. "You want to tell me about it?"

"Well, we had sixty couples, plus some friends in a room about the size——"

"No, I mean the marriage, not the wedding."

"Oh," said the woman. "Well, it happened because of a horrible mistake. Some time ago I was to elope with the boy I loved. He was studying Civil Engineering, majoring in Sewage and Solid Wastes. 'There's waste in money and money in waste,' he'd always tell me. Anyway, my father, a widower, coincidentally was eloping, too."

"How long had he been a widower?" asked Lou.

"Oh, my mother passed on when I was a little girl," said the woman. "Choked to death on Shredded Wheat."

"All right, go on."

"Well, my father was eloping with a notorious woman who lived in our town. The kind of woman who fed pigeons in her nightgown, who sat in chairs without legs—I'm sure you know the type. I hated her."

"You'd met her in person?"

"Yes. Once. She threw bottle caps at me."

"And she was eloping with your father."

"As fate would have it, he and I were leaving on the same night. There was an electrical storm, a power blackout, a mixup in the cars, and before anyone knew what happened, my sweetheart married that dreadful woman and I wound up with Daddy."

Lou leaned back in his chair. "Incredible, to put it mildly."

"And the terrible part is, my sweetheart and this dreadful woman have a wonderful marriage. He has his own company now, United Sewage, and they're branching out into cesspools and septic tanks. The urinal division alone grossed three million dollars last year. And she has her own pigeon coop, and a special carpenter who saws the legs off her chairs."

"And you and your father?"

The woman looked aside. "Daddy and I haven't had a happy day together in six years."

"Have you tried a marriage counselor?"

She shook her head yes. "The marriage, of course, has never been consummated."

"Smart move," said Lou.

"But I was young and attractive," said the woman.

"A good combo."

"I knew my share of bellboys, jockeys, demolition men, shepherds, executioners, and a few dry cleaners."

"That's what happens when you're young and attractive."

"I'm afraid it's not a pretty picture," said the woman.

"Oh, don't blame yourself," said Lou. "The marriage just didn't go."

"Daddy took as much as he could, and then left," said the woman.

"Was he well-to-do, your father?"

"He was penniless, and in poor health."

"Heart?"

"Yes. He had stones."

"Stones are usually in the kidneys or gall bladder."

"Daddy had heart stones. Sometimes he'd just grab his chest and double over, and I'd know: Daddy was passing a stone. Sometimes, this would happen even if we walked by a loose boulder."

"When he left, did you search for him?"

"Yes. I wanted to find him to divorce him and try it over as his daughter again." She wiped away a tear. Lou handed her his handkerchief, which she looked at, and then quickly returned. "I'm sorry, this is . . . not clean."

Lou quickly pocketed it.

"I traced him as far as San Francisco," said the woman, "and then lost him."

"I understand," said Lou. "If I can just have his name." He picked up his pen.

"Vladimir Tserijemiwtz."

Lou looked at her. "Vladimir Tserijemiwtz. Has a nice lilt. How do you spell that?"

"I'm not sure," said the woman. "We were never that close."

"That's understandable," said Lou, getting up.

"It's not like he was my uncle," said the woman. "Or my broker."

"Why don't we just leave everything in my hands," said Lou.

"Can you hold it all?"

"Oh, yes. Sure. I'll get in touch with you in a few days."

She rose, and he led her to the door. "Do you have any money?" he asked.

"Daddy left a ten-thousand-dollar trust fund for each of us girls, but as his wife I can't touch it."

Lou took a bill from his pocket. "Here's a twenty."

"Oh, Mr. Peckinpaugh, you shouldn't."

"You're right," said Lou. "But I want you to go to a beauty parlor and get that cheap dye job washed out."

"What?"

"And then, when you're ready to tell me the truth, *Mrs. Montenegro,* call me. I'm getting sick and tired of playing 'Guess what the fruitcake's name is today.' "

"Is there another game you'd prefer," said the woman weakly, almost visibly shrinking. "Dominoes? Potsy?"

"No games," said Lou.

"You're still sore about me upchucking on your trench coat, aren't you?"

"I've seen better shows of friendship," said Lou, "but no, that's not it."

"Then what? Just because that first story was a little untrue—"

"You're good, baby," said Lou, "but you're not good enough. I know who you're looking for and why you want to find him. Only from now on, it's anybody's ball game."

"You know . . . everything?"

"Not everything. I can't bake a grasshopper pie or blow glass. But I know enough to advise you to lay low. It's possible Blubber and his delightful boy killed Floyd, and they'd like to see you out of the way."

The woman looked startled. "Me? Naw. Me?" She shook her head. "But I'm harmless."

"So were four other dead people in the hotel with Floyd."

"Well . . . what should I do, then?"

"To begin with, don't call me for three days, and

135

when you do, use your real name. By the way, what is it?"

The woman lowered her eyes. "Mary Jones."

Lou looked at her. "You never quit, do you?"

"I swear it, Lou."

"A woman shouldn't swear."

"My name is Mary Jones."

Lou held the door open, and the woman walked out. "Change it," he yelled after her. "It sounds phony."

He closed the door . . . and gasped. There, in the middle of the room was Pepe Damascus, pointing a small, pearl-handled revolver at Lou's throat.

"You will be so kind as to put your hands on top of your head."

Lou stood frozen.

"Move!" said Pepe.

"You didn't say, 'Simon Says,'" said Lou, but he complied. "How'd you get in here, I didn't even smell you?"

Damascus grinned. "There are ways that those trained in Oriental disciplines can deceive men's minds."

"But you're not from the Orient."

"So what. There's other ways also. You could be from Los Angeles and still trick people. Especially women."

"All right," said Lou. "What do you want, pip-squeak? I'm busy."

Damascus grinned. "You will accompany me to Mr. Jasper Blubber's suite."

"For what purpose?"

"To be disposed of. We have decided that you are no longer of any use to us." He giggled maniacally, all teeth and gums.

Lou shook his head.

"Isn't that the worst laugh you ever heard?" said Damascus.

"It's right up there in the top ten," said Lou.

Suddenly, the door opened and Bess came in. Lou still had his hands on top of his head. Pepe held the revolver leveled at Lou's throat.

"Hi!" said Bess.

"Hi," said Lou.

"Hello," said Damascus.

"Lieutenant DiMaggio on the phone, Lou," said Bess. "Oh, I didn't know you were being held up. Sorry."

"That's all right," said Lou. "It's business. Tell DiMaggio I'll be in Mr. Jasper Blubber's suite at— uh—" He turned to Damascus. "Where's he staying again?"

"Crusades."

"—the Crusades Hotel," continued Lou. "A Mr. Pepe Damascus is taking me there now. I think they intend to do away with me."

"Go away with you?" said Bess.

"No, *do* away with me. As in 'terminate my vital functions.' Now, you got all that?"

"Right," said Bess, turning and walking out the door. She closed it behind her.

"Very efficient," said Lou.

Damascus looked puzzled. A droplet of oil from one of his ringlets ran down over his cheek. "I don't think I handled that very well," he said.

Lou nodded. "Crime," he said. "Crime is a very complicated business. A chess game, really. The well-executed crime has the beauty of a mathematical proof. There are fundamental symmetries about it, progressions based on ineluctable logic, a twisting and elusive inevitability. You really have to think things out first."

Damascus contorted his face, annoyed with him-

137

self. Why did he always screw up at the last minute? He could spend months negotiating the smuggling of raw opium for processing into the purest heroin, then mistakenly deliver fifty kilos of the finished product to a store that sold children's shoes. He'd once meticulously planned a bank robbery, then was unable to park the get-away car outside because he'd forgotten a dime for the meter.

"You have to keep your eye on the goal," said Lou.

"I know, I know," said Damascus. "I'm always so busy greasing my hair, it keeps slipping my mind."

Gently, Lou removed the gun from Pepe's hand. He led him to the side door by which he'd apparently gained entrance. "Look, don't feel badly," said Lou. "There are some people who commit crimes for years and get no recognition. And even if you do commit one successful robbery, or an embezzlement, there's no guarantee you'll pull off more. All you can do is your best, and hope that that's good enough." He placed a hand on Pepe's shoulder. "You feel a little better?"

Damascus nodded.

"Now go back to Blubber," said Lou, "and tell him how I just outfoxed you."

Damascus frowned. "When I tell him, he will pull my arms out from the sockets, soak me in gasoline and set me on fire, chop my legs off at the knees, and split my skull with an ax."

"Tough boss," said Lou.

"Then he will kill me," said Damascus.

"Well," said Lou, deciding on levity, "what's a funny-looking guy like you wanna grow old for, anyway?" He opened the door, and felt a brief pang of compassion. "I'm sorry."

"It's all right," said Damascus. "I thrive on abuse. It's like feeding garbage to a goat."

"It's just . . . I think you and I could've been friends, if you were an entirely different person."

Damascus stepped through the door. "Oh, well," he said, "at least I won't have to listen to this voice any more."

Lou closed the door. He put Damascus's gun in his pocket and crossed to the outer office. Bess was still on the phone when he entered the room.

"Right! Right! I'll tell him."

She hung up.

"Mrs. O'Brien, your landlady."

Lou smacked himself in the forehead. "Of course! Dummy! I knew it. Rent, right? I meant to give it to her, and it just slipped my mind. I owe three months now; she'll kill me. Gee, I'm getting like Damascus. I wonder if she'll evict me. Can she evict me? I'll hide. If I hide, they can't find me, and if they can't find me, they can't evict me. Where should—"

"Lou!"

"Where should I hide? I don't know where to hide. A hotel costs too much. Wait, I'll hide in the apartment. I'll stay in the closet and pretend I'm a shirt. Oh wait, the moths, I—"

"Lou, for God's sake!"

Lou took a deep breath. "What?"

"Lou, it's got nothing to do with the rent," said Bess. "Nothing. She didn't even bring it up."

"Not the rent?" said Lou, dazedly. "Then . . ." He thought intently. "Was it the leaky pipe in the kitchen? They're complaining again downstairs? Mrs. Zuckerman and her daughter, Eileen, the one with the pet waterbug? Well, I had a plumber estimate—"

"Lou, it wasn't the pipe."

"The water buffalo? I gave that away. And the siren I don't even use any more. Was it those? Was it the time I went pee-pee in the hall? I didn't—"

139

"She said someone just broke into your apartment. She thinks they're still there."

Lou smiled and slumped in relief. "That's all? That's all she wanted? Oh, thank God."

"But there's an intruder in your apartment," said Bess. "Doesn't that bother you?"

"Naw," said Lou. "Nobody can survive in that place for long. Besides, it means I'm making a lot of people nervous."

"Including Mrs. O'Brien," said Bess.

But Lou had already left the office.

In his apartment house, Lou walked slowly up the stairs and cautiously pushed open the door at the stairwell landing. The hall was empty, and it seemed quieter than usual. Lou removed Pepe's pistol from his pocket and advanced toward his apartment. An ant ran across his path, followed by a roach, a mouse, a cat, and an alligator. A moment later, a large waterbug appeared, chasing them all. "And they got the nerve to complain about me," muttered Lou. He continued on. When he reached his apartment, he placed his finger on the gun's trigger and inhaled deeply. Carefully, he nudged open the door.

IX

Bess tried the library first. As soon as she'd seen the name, VLADIMIR TSERIJEMIWTZ, she'd known that no simple anagramatic rearrangement would be satisfactory. It was too obvious, and too susceptible to solution by someone really intent on getting the answer. She went to the main library on State Street and approached a clerk in the reference section.

"I wonder if you could help me. I'm interested in systematic approaches to the solving of anagrams. Maybe something mathematical, even. But it has to involve non-obvious, formalistic procedures."

The clerk stared at her blankly. "Have you tried the card catalogue?"

"This isn't a card catalogue type of problem," said Bess, impatiently.

"Well, I'm just a clerk," said the clerk. "My job is to tell people to use the card catalogue and to say, 'No talking, please, this is a library.' You want anything else, you'll have to see the head librarian."

"Let's go," said Bess.

They wended their way down a staircase and then through a group of basement offices before stopping outside a paneled enclosure. "Wait here," said the clerk, as he went inside.

A moment later, he emerged. "Mr. Snodley will see you now."

Bess went in.

Leaning back in a chair behind a large desk, a fortyish man in a business suit smiled pleasantly. He had many teeth missing. "How do," he said, looking Bess over carefully. "Mr. Ingram told me your problem. Shut the door, please."

Bess closed the door.

"Rather specialized area for a young lady," said Snodley.

Bess noticed a bit of saliva foam appear on his lips. "It's an assignment I have," she said.

"Graduate school?" said Snodley.

"Uh, no. From my boss."

"What line is *he* in? I mean, he must do well to employ such an attractive secretary."

Bess glanced down at his desk. She thought she could see an open issue of *National Geographic*. "Mr. Snodley, I'm in quite a hurry. Can you help me?"

Snodley rose and approached her. Before she could even think, he'd placed an arm on her shoulder. "Yes, I can help you," he said. Saliva dripped from a corner of his mouth.

Bess backed away.

"It's specialized information," said Snodley. "Look, you don't get that for nothing."

"No dice," said Bess.

"Oh, come on," said Snodley. "You have lust written all over you. Come on." He attempted to hug her, but Bess wriggled away. She managed to pry the door open.

"Please," said Snodley, as she stood in the doorway. "A librarian doesn't get much. I spent half the day searching for pictures of naked cannibals."

"I'm sorry," said Bess, stepping out. "I'm saving myself for my lover."

"I'll make a deposit in your account," said Snodley.

Bess began to walk away.

"All right!" yelled the librarian. "There's nothing here. Go see Professor Calvin Emory at the University. He can help you."

Bess smiled and mouthed "Thank you." On the way out, she passed a mirror and noticed that someone had written tiny words all over the back and sides of her dress. Must've happened on the cable car coming here, she thought. Funny, she hadn't felt a thing. She leaned closer and saw that the words were all the same. LUST. So that's what Snodley had meant, she realized.

An hour later, she was in the Mathematics Department office of the University of San Francisco.

"I phoned before," she told the secretary. "Here to see Professor Emory."

"Oh, go right in," said the receptionist. "Professor Emory's board meeting just finished."

Bess entered the office and introduced herself to the professor, a lean, wiry, balding man who smoked a pipe. Carefully, she outlined the problem to him. Emory nodded thoughtfully.

"Of course," he said "there is a strong temptation to think of this only as a problem in combinatorial mathematics. For example, consider a last name. 'Vladimir Tserijemiwtz' has twenty letters. If we rule out names of one letter, we are talking about the sum of any permutation of twenty letters taken two at a time plus twenty letters taken three at a time, four at a time, et cetera, until we get to twenty letters taken twenty at a time."

Bess looked dejected. "This is over my head," she said. "I can barely tell time."

"Each permutation group," continued the professor, "is given by n factorial, where n is twenty in this case, divided by the quantity n minus r, factorial, where r progressively assumes the values two, three, four . . . until twenty. Wanna fuck?"

"I think I'd better for— What?"

"I just threw that in for amusement," said the professor. "Also your dress . . ."

Bess glanced down. "Someone did that," she said. "I couldn't remove it. Look, where is all this leading?"

"If we were twenty years in the future," said Emory, "I'd say, let's program a computer with a simple algorithm and compare results to the phone book. In seconds, we'd reduce the problem to tolerable dimensions. However, no existing machine today is capable of handling this type of data. Plus—and here, really, is the point—this is *not* a coding problem. What you need is an expert in cryptography. Someone with a knowledge of foreign languages, and an uncanny ability to sense certain patterns and repetitions. Someone who can rearrange chaos and make order. Someone with an intuition so specialized that he probably excludes all other areas of human existence. A very unusual individual, all in all."

"And where might I find such a person," asked Bess sweetly.

Emory sucked on his pipe. He grinned. "You know, a mathematics professor doesn't get much," he said.

"Don't say any more," said Bess.

"Try the army," said Emory. "Office of Cryptography. They have someone there named Wunga. Never met the chap, but he's supposed to be brilliant beyond belief."

"Thanks," said Bess.

"I'll just play with my permutations," said Emory sadly.

The room was in a small sub-basement. Bess had been escorted through the narrow corridors by a Lieutenant; their footsteps echoed eerily as they walked.

"Hardly anyone comes here," said the Lieutenant. "Really hush-hush deal, this place. You must have quite a bit of pull, lady."

"Well, the Colonel seemed to think I pulled adequately," said Bess demurely.

"You just go right in," said the Lieutenant. "Give him the problem, and then wait. Supposedly, there has never been a problem of any kind—in coding, that is —that he couldn't solve in less than five minutes."

Bess thanked him, and the Lieutenant left.

The sign over the door said simply WUNGA. Bess knocked, and waited. She knocked again. When there was no answer, she pushed open the door and let herself in. Inside, the room was completely bare except for a cot in one corner and a high, wooden stool in the center. On the stool sat a hunched-over figure. There were no windows.

"Mr. Wunga?" said Bess tentatively.

Wunga looked up. His hair was combed straight down and almost reached his eyebrows; his ears stuck way out from his head. He had a hairy, protruding jaw and gross overbite. His nostrils were the largest Bess had ever seen. When he formed his mouth into a slack, twitching grin, there could be no doubt. Wunga was an idiot.

Or more likely, Bess thought, an idiot-savant, one of those peculiar individuals who could perform unusual mental feats in one area, and one area only, and were defective in most every other facet of ilfe. Just as Emory had postulated! Only this, clearly, was an extreme. One of nature's end-points, a cosmic jest.

Bess stared at him. "Mr. Wunga? Colonel Brooks said that you might be able to help me."

Wunga looked at her dully.

"Mr. Wunga?"

Wunga's eyes began to close.

"Mr. Wunga, please. You're my last hope."

She removed the piece of paper with the name on it, and held it up for the idiot-savant to see. Desperately, not knowing whether he was hearing, or understanding, she stated the problem. Wunga's eyes fluttered open and, very briefly, he appeared to look at the page. He began to rock slightly on his stool and then started to rub his right thigh with his left hand. After a moment, his hand movements extended upward to his groin.

"Mr. Wunga?" said Bess. "Mr. Wunga, can you hear me? Did you understand the problem?"

Slowly, Wunga opened his mouth. His tongue seemed to loll on his lower teeth. A thick, sluggish sound began to come from his throat.

"Wuh—"

"What?"

"Wun. . . ."

Bess strained to hear.

"Wunga."

"Yes?"

"Wunga have answer."

"You have—oh, Mr. Wunga!" Bess felt a hot flush of genuine excitement. She smiled broadly and, in an impulsive gesture, touched the idiot's hand. "Mr. Wunga, that's fantastic, absolutely fantastic. How did you—?" She shook her head. "Never mind, I'm sure I wouldn't understand. Just . . . tell it to me." She shut her eyes for an instant, waiting for the revelation.

146

After a moment, when there was silence, she opened them again.

The idiot's mouth hung loosely opened, the eyes blankly staring. Only the hand still worked back and forth.

"Wun. . . ." he said slowly.

"Yes?"

"Wunga."

"Go on," said Bess, "I'm listening." She breathed heavily.

Something glistened in the idiot's pupils; he focused on Bess's legs. "Wunga no get much," he said.

The curtains were drawn, and the room was in total darkness. Lou stood in the doorway and tried to let his eyes grow accustomed to the lack of illumination. Suddenly, the overhead light went on, and he turned automatically to the side. (This was a reflex he had that seemed to serve no purpose whatsoever. Whenever someone switched on a light, even overhead, he automatically turned to the side.) Sitting in the armchair, her hand on the lamp chain, was Marlene. She wore a long and very clinging white evening gown. Her hair hung down her back, reaching nearly to her waist. Lou stared at her.

"Well, looka here. If it isn't Mrs. DuChard herself. I expected a housebreaker, and instead I find a heartbreaker."

"Lou, don't—"

"Wearing the same dress I bought for you Bastille Day in that little shop near the café where we had turtle soup and Cokes every afternoon, and the waiter's name was Sheldon."

"Lou, don't—"

"Tell me, do you still go dancing in that smoky little club where the men and women used the same john?"

"They never used the same john."

"They didn't? Gee, I saw several women—never mind. Do you?"

"Oh, Lou—"

"Moving your body next to his, slowly around the floor. And then the walls, and the—"

"Don't say those things to me, Lou."

"Who should I say them to? My radiator? Dancing closer to the bandstand so you can hear the music, and singing into his ear, 'Hi ho, hi ho, it's off to work we go'?"

"Stop it, Lou!" shrieked Marlene. She held her hands up to her ears. "Stop it!"

Lou, who'd been shouting, relaxed somewhat. With a sneaky gesture, Marlene removed a tiny piece of earwax with her pinky.

"Does he hold you the way I did?" asked Lou plaintively.

"Oh, Lou . . . please."

"Does he run his fingers through your hair the way I did?"

Marlene twisted uncomfortably in her seat.

"Do his lips press against yours the way yours pressed against mine?"

Marlene bit her lower lip. Then she bit her upper lip, and finally, her nose.

"Does he know you as a woman the way *I* knew you and held you and loved you like no other woman I ever knew before? Does he? I want to know. *Tell me!*"

Marlene sat up. "Yes!" she screamed. "Yes! Yes! Yes! *Yes! Yes!*"

Lou turned away. "Why do you say things like that to hurt me? Is it because of that time with the cucumber and the cold cream?"

Marlene shook her head no. "Do you think *I* have no feelings? All day long I sweat and slave over a hot stove and when you come home do you ever offer to

148

take me out? Anywhere? I cook for you and clean for—"

"What the hell are you talking about?"

"Wait a minute," said Marlene, composing herself. "Wait. That was a different argument. All right, here goes. Do you think I have no memories?"

" I think you have a great set," said Lou.

"I said *mem*ories," repeated Marlene. "Did you think my heart didn't stop that night in the club when I saw you standing there . . . wearing that same, sweet, rumpled shirt that hasn't been laundered in a thousand nights?"

Lou let his mind drift back. "I almost forgot what you looked like," he said softly. "Day by day I erased your face in my mind, little by little, until all I had left was your right ear and three front teeth on the bottom. Two canines and a molar, I think."

"I still carry your picture in my locket," said Marlene.

"You do? But what if—"

"Naturally, I had to cut off your head in case Paul found it."

Lou was touched. "Does he know about us?"

"What do you mean? He knows me, and he knows you exist."

"No, I mean us."

"You mean how we were in Lyon?"

"I meant," said Lou, a bit sheepish, "in Marseilles. You remember? When we bought the wet suits? And the chicken fat?"

Marlene nodded. "Paul is a clever man, but naïve in so many ways. Despite all he's been through, he said to me the other day, 'Down deep, I believe Hitler's probably an all-right guy.' "

"Down deep is where he belongs," said Lou.

"Anyway," said Marlene, "Paul suspected something the other night. When we got home he asked me if

149

there was anything between me and Tinker."

But Lou's mind had drifted again, back in time, back all those years. "Suddenly," he said, "it all seems as though it were yesterday."

"It does? To me, even yesterday doesn't seem like yesterday. It seems like never."

"I stood in that train station waiting for you for over six hours. And then your letter came—"

"To the train station?"

"To my hotel. And I read it outside and it started to rain. I opened the letter and the ink ran all over the page. The most important letter of my life and I still don't know what the hell it said."

"What the hell it said was this," said Marlene. 'Dear Louis, I love you more than life itself, but to run off with you now that my country is in danger would be an act of cowardice. I am marrying Paul DuChard because. . . .' And that's all I can remember."

Lou was nonplussed. *"You can't remember why you married him?"*

Marlene gazed at the ceiling. "That letter was written a long time ago."

"But still—"

"I've written *thousands* of letters since. Why, my correspondence with the phone company alone must— But what's the difference, Louis? What's done is done."

Lou turned away and began muttering to himself. "Can't remember why she married him. I must've gone through eight liquor stores."

"Lou," called Marlene. "Enough muttering. No schizoid withdrawal symptoms now."

Lou whirled back. "Don't you have a copy of the letter? Don't you keep copies?"

"I keep only what's in my heart," said Marlene. "A few auricles, a few ventricles, some valves—and you. You've never left it."

"I see," said Lou. "Did you ever stop to worry that I might've killed myself over you?"

"And if you had," said Marlene, dramatically, "it would have been easier than what I went through."

Lou raised his eyebrows.

"Sleeping night after night with a man I didn't really love."

"I don't really think that's in the same league with being dead," scoffed Lou. "When you're dead, you can't even hear a ballgame."

"Feeling his hands on my skin," continued Marlene, "watching me undress, taking baths and showers with me, making me wear all sorts of—"

"All right!" shouted Lou. And then, more softly, "I got the picture. I heard it, let's get on to something new."

"How about people in the news?" suggested Marlene.

"No."

"Mail-order businesses?"

"I mean something involving us."

Marlene looked at him with pleading eyes. "I want to come back, Lou."

"Oh, Jesus."

"I want to start over again, to pick up the pieces of our broken lives."

"My pieces are in the garbage."

"To be with you, to love you, to take care of you . . ."

"Just like that, huh?" said Lou, cynically.

"Well, I would want to redecorate this room. I don't like that green sofa very much."

"Do you mean it?" said Lou suddenly, beginning to melt. "You and me, just the way it was?"

"Not the way it was. Better! Better, Lou!"

Lou paused. "How could it be better than it was?"

Marlene chuckled. "I know more now, Lou. Paul

has taught me so much. You give me a few ice cubes and a knotted handkerchief, and I can do things with my mouth that—"

"I don't want to hear about it!" said Lou angrily. "Maybe some day you can write it out, but I don't want to get this verbally. Let's keep it the way it was."

"All right," said Marlene. "The way it was. I have to acquiesce."

"There's a bathroom inside," said Lou.

"Do you have any champagne?" asked Marlene.

Lou nodded. "I still have the bottle I was saving for our honeymoon."

Marlene sighed.

"I have the bread and cheese, too," added Lou, "but it's hard as a rock." He walked toward the kitchen. "I'll be right back."

In the kitchen, he crossed to the refrigerator, opened it, and removed a bottle of champagne. Only then did he catch sight of the figure seated at the table.

"Need any help, Fred?" said Betty.

She wore a beret and raincoat, and puffed languorously on a cigarette. A suitcase rested on the floor next to her.

"What are you doing here?" said Lou.

She cocked her head. "Is that any way to greet me?"

"Well, it's better than throwing a jar of sour cream at your shoes. Now what's doing?"

"I missed my boat."

"It doesn't sail until tomorrow."

Betty shrugged. "So I missed it early. The ticket said yesterday."

"There must've been some mix-up," said Lou. Then, remembering the situation, he lowered his voice. "You can't stay here. There's something going on. I'm busy picking up the pieces of my life."

"If it's just a piece you want," said Betty seductively, "you can pick it up right here."

Lou looked around. "I want you out of this apartment. I'll manage to get her into the bathroom, and that's your signal to go."

"And if I refuse?"

"I'll hammer a nail directly into your face."

"I'd like that, Lou."

He stared at her coldly. "Sometimes, it doesn't pay to treat a dame like you nice."

He started for the door.

"You'll be back," said Betty smugly.

"What makes you think so?" said Lou.

"My analysis of your sense of responsibility."

"Uh-uh."

"My knowledge of your real feelings for me."

Lou shook his head. The bottle of champagne felt cold in his hands.

"My perception that you forgot the glasses."

Lou grunted, and grabbed two dusty goblets from the cupboard. Turning, he left the room. In the living area, Marlene was rearranging the furniture.

"I think this chair works much better over here, don't you?" she asked.

Lou shrugged.

"Oh, Louis, I can't wait to give my first party."

"Swell," said Lou unenthusiastically. "Anything you want." He popped the cork from the champagne bottle.

"French?" asked Marlene.

"Domestic," said Lou, studying the bottle. "It says it's from one of the finest vineyards in all Detroit." He poured into each goblet.

Marlene tooks hers and sniffed. "Smells peculiar," she said. "Like from gasoline.'

"Let's drink to us, kid," said Lou, "and the way it was."

Marlene lifted her glass. "And here's thanking you

153

for when you steal the papers from Colonel Schlissel and then seeing that—"

"Wait a minute! Wait a minute. *What?*"

"Seeing that Paul is safely out of San Francisco," continued Marlene.

Lou squeezed the glass then with so much force that it shattered in his hands. Thin trickles of blood formed tiny rivulets on his palms.

"Is it something I said?" inquired Marlene.

Lou glared at her. "So that's it! That's why you came up here tonight with your bedroom eyes and your dining-room lips."

"Oh, Lou—"

"Playing me for a sap, and all the while you were just using me to get your French-fried husband out of the fat."

"No! No, Louis, that's not the way it is."

"It is the way it is."

"Is not."

"Is."

"Is not."

"Okay, then explain it to me," said Lou.

"I want to tell you everything," said Marlene. "Everything, darling, but not tonight."

"Not tonight? When, next Tuesday? In your memoirs? In your next life?"

"Oh Lou, please, let's save tonight for us."

"It's too late."

"Let's make love," said Marlene, "the way we did that weekend at the Hotel Josephine."

"We can't," said Lou flatly. "In the first place I don't have the chains, the leather straps, or the whipped cream. And in the second, we never stayed at the Hotel Josephine."

Marlene scoffed. Then she coughed and sneezed. "Of course, we did. That charming little country hotel, you don't remember, *ma chérie?*"

154

"No."

"The big red mirrors on the closet door, and you turned them toward the bed, and I said, 'Oh Paul—' " Lou sneered.

"Sorry," said Marlene. "My mistake." She turned her gaze away from him. "It was an awful place. I couldn't wait to leave."

Lou, anguished, put down his drink and walked over to a wall. He leaned his shoulder against it and began to sob. After a moment he started to bang his head into the plaster.

"Come in!" said Marlene, who had not been looking.

"I *am* in," said Lou.

"Oh, Lou," she said, turning, "you must feel—"

"Crushed," he said. "It's not a good way to drive in nails. Look, Marlene, excuse me. I'm upset. I think I need a couple of aspirins."

He walked to the bathroom and went inside, closing the door behind him. He was shocked to see Georgia, still in mourning black, sitting on the edge of the tub. She looked up at him with pleading eyes and imploring earlobes.

"Who is she, Lou?"

He quickly motioned her to lower her voice. "What the hell are you doing here?" he whispered urgently.

"I want to know who she is."

"Georgia, will you please . . ."

She stood up and tugged at his shirt. "You said you'd call me. Why didn't you call?"

"I was busy."

"I even missed Floyd's funeral because I didn't want to leave the phone. I haven't even gone to the bathroom in two days for fear of missing your call."

"Well, you're in one now," said Lou. He looked around warily. "You didn't bring the cops with you again, did you?" He reached over and quickly pulled back the shower curtain. No one was there.

Georgia removed a small jar from her pocketbook. "I had him cremated. That's all that's left of him, Lou." She unscrewed the top of the jar. "Look! I always thought of him as a bigger man."

Lou looked inside. "What, uh, kind of a jar was it?" he asked.

"Kind? What kind? A glass jar. It was made of glass."

"No what had been in it?" said Lou.

"Oh," said Georgia, nodding. "Well, gherkins, I think. Yes, I believe it was a gherkin jar."

"So," said Lou, philosophically, clicking his tongue. "My friend goes to his final resting place among the pickles. I hope he finds tranquillity."

"There may still be some shreds of sauerkraut in there" said Georgia. Suddenly, she thrust the jar at Lou.

"Don't do that, Georgia."

"But it's for you, Lou."

He held the jar, feeling acutely uncomfortable.

"You keep him," said Georgia, softly. "He was your partner."

"No, no," said Lou, handing back the jar. "He was your husband. He belongs on your mantelpiece."

"Lou, he doesn't go well, he doesn't fit in with the décor—"

"The hell with the décor!"

"Oh, Lou" said Georgia, half hysterical. "I don't want him, I want you! He's so gray and smoky and shrivelly, and you're pink and fleshy. He's burned-out chunks, and you're a hunk. Oh God, I'm so crazy about you!"

"Georgia, please—"

She flung herself at him then, kissing him frantically and pawing at his body, and licking his shirt sleeves.

"Watch it!" he yelled suddenly. "Watch it, you're spilling Floyd!" Clutching at her dress, he managed to pull her off him.

"Take me away, Lou," she begged. "Please take me away."

"Stop pleading, Georgia."

"Bleeding? I'm not bleeding."

"I said *pleading*. As in begging, sucking up."

Her face hardened. "Take me away from here, or I swear I'll tell the cops how you and Floyd fought over me. It wouldn't take much to pin his killing on you. . . ."

Lou took a deep breath. Blackmail, in all its forms, was not exactly new to him. "I'll discuss it with you in a few minutes. Screw Floyd back on."

He hurried out of the bathroom and closed the door behind him.

In the living room, Marlene was putting on her gloves. "I'm going, Louis," she said.

One down, thought Lou. Change from a three-ring circus to two.

"It was wrong of me to come here," said Marlene, "and try to resurrect the past."

"Resurrections are tough," acknowledged Lou.

"What was, was, and will never be 'was' again."

"And what is, is," said Lou philosophically, "and 'is' only for the moment, or until a rash appears."

Marlene started for the door.

And suddenly, with all his being, Lou knew that he'd lost her once and was not going to lose her again. "Wait!" he said hoarsely. "I lost you once, I'm not gonna lose you again."

She paused.

"I don't know how," he continued, "but I'll get those papers from Schlissel. You and your husband meet me at the Oakland Ferry at nine o'clock tomorrow night."

"Could we make it ten?" said Marlene. "I have a beauty parlor appointment."

"Nine," said Lou sternly. "Once he's on board the boat, I give him the papers and you give him the air."

157

"The shaft, you mean," said Marlene.

"Look, there's no turning back now, angel. And then it's you and me."

"The two of us."

"Just the way it was."

"Only better."

"I told you," said Lou loudly, "I don't want it better! Don't you know too much of a good thing, and God strikes you down. Gives you a vicious liver ailment out of left field, or makes a fungus thrive in your inner ear. The idea is everything in moderation, nothing to excess, then God doesn't notice you. He gets people who make money in stocks, instead."

"Waste not, want not," said Marlene.

"All right," said Lou. "Look, you've missed the point. Now get out of here, I got work to do."

They crossed to the door, and Lou opened it. Marlene, facing Lou, did not see Bess standing just outside in the hall.

"Lou," said Marlene, "all those years you waited for me—was there ever another girl?"

"Never," said Lou, "although I occasionally read a filthy magazine."

Bess waved from the hall. "Hello, Lou! I came as fast as I could."

Marlene whirled. She stared, bewildered, at Bess. "I see," she said slowly, turning back to Lou. "Did I ever tell you about the time Paul and I were in the back of his Citroën—"

"Don't tell me those things!" said Lou. "It's not what you think."

"Then what is it? Is this your landlady? Your cousin? A health inspector?"

"She's my secretary," said Lou. "It's a completely business relationship."

"Oh," said Marlene sheepishly. "I apologize then, I—"

"I'll see you tomorrow night at the ferry," snapped Lou.

"I'll bring along some wallpapers for you to pick out," said Marlene. She walked through the door and headed down the stairs.

"I'm sorry to interrupt you, Lou," said Bess, "but I did it, and thought you should know."

"Did what?"

"I unscrambled the name."

X

Lou's eyes lit up. Thank God, he thought. At last, a break. First one, on this case. "Good girl," he said. "Wait here, I'll be right back."

He closed the door, leaving her hurt, surprised and confused. Also rubbing her nose. He quickly crossed to the kitchen and opened the door.

"Come here!"

Betty came out.

"Maybe you're right, Slinky. Maybe you and I are one of a kind."

She smiled expectantly.

"I'm getting out of here tomorrow night, and I'm taking you with me."

"Oh, Fred! Oh, darling!"

"But I want you to do something for me first."

"I love it when you give me orders," said Betty.

"Say, do you like spanking? You know, I lie across your lap, and you lift up my dress and paddle my tush until I scream for mercy, but you keep—"

"No deviations now," said Lou. "I want you to arrange to meet Schlissel in the club tonight."

"What if he won't come?"

"Use your feminine wiles."

"I don't think I have any more wiles. What are they, anyway? Are they something like tampons?"

"I'm not sure," said Lou. "I think they're similar to spoils. Anyway, tell him I said I'd deliver DuChard if he turns the papers over to me."

"How do you know he'll bring them?"

"He'll bring them all right. When he does, I want you to get him to dance with you."

"I don't think he's too light on his feet," said Betty.

"Doesn't matter," said Lou. "While you're dancing, you go into your magic fingers routine." He led her to the door. "I'll meet you at the Oakland Ferry at nine o'clock, got that?"

"Nine o'clock," repeated Betty. "Couldn't we make it eight? Nine o'clock my favorite radio program is on, the *Lone Ranger*."

"Nine," said Lou. "Bring the papers with you." He opened the door; Bess was still standing outside. "And then," he said to Betty, "it's a slow boat to China for you and me, kid. Now get out of here, I got work to do."

"Don't wear yourself out," said Betty. "I've saving that for me."

"I'll still have a little left," said Lou, grinning.

Betty turned to Bess. "Hi!"

"Hello," said Bess.

"See you tomorrow, Fred," said Betty to Lou.

"I'm his secretary," explained Bess.

"I have no clear relationship to him," said Betty, "although right now I'm happy with a murky one."

She strode down the hall and disappeared down the staircase.

"Why does she call you Fred?" asked Bess.

"Long story," said Lou. "Okay, what have you got?"

Bess shrugged, a casual gesture belying her excitement. She removed a piece of paper from her handbag. "Here it is, Lou."

Lou stared at the paper.

"And wait'll you hear who it turns out to be. . . ."

Bess started into the apartment, but Lou gently shoved her back into the hall, using a *Choong-dan Makgi* to the solar plexus. "Hold it a second," he said. "I'll be right with you."

He closed the door in her face, quickly crossed the living room, and barged into the bathroom. There he found Georgia, sobbing, holding the empty jar of ashes over the toilet.

"Georgia, you—"

"I tripped over the mat," cried Georgia. "I couldn't help it."

Lou shook his head. "You really should be more careful. You know falls in the bathroom are the number one cause of household injury."

"Oh, Lou," moaned Georgia. "He's in there . . . that's Floyd, Lou." She stared disconsolately into the bowl.

"All right," said Lou, "get a hold of yourself. I'd recommend a hammer-lock or a half-nelson. There's no point crying over spilt husbands." And with a swift, decisive motion, he flushed the john.

Georgia began to moan. Gradually, the moans escalated to wails, the wails to screams, the screams to high-pitched, maniacal shrieks. Georgia was hysterical.

"I guess this is the wrong time to say a prayer," noted Lou.

"Now I have no one!" shrieked Georgia. "Only you."

162

She turned to Lou and suddenly lowered her voice. "And if I can't have you, no one will."

From the folds of her dress, she pulled out a revolver. "This is a revolver," she said.

"Are you crazy?" said Lou, knowing, of course, that she was, and carefully measuring the distance between them. "Put that away."

She cocked the hammer.

Lou knew he needed something to divert her. "That's no revolver," he said. "That's . . . the coccyx of a lemming."

"What? The co—"

He lunged and caught her wrist. She beat at his face with her free hand as he twisted his back to her, concentrating his efforts on shaking loose the gun. She pounded his head, his neck, and his spine. He couldn't loosen her grip, though he savaged her wrist with his nails.

"You . . . really . . . should . . . cut . . . those," she said through clenched teeth, just as the gun went off. The bullet hissed as it entered the water in the bowl.

"Oh, God!" said Georgia plaintively, her hand finally going limp and dropping the revolver. "We shot Floyd again."

Lou kicked the gun over to the bathtub. "He's past all of that now."

Georgia nodded sadly. "That was some crazy remark you made."

"When? You mean about Floyd being past hurting."

"No, I mean about the coccyx of a lemming. That's not quite a sane thing to say."

She shoots her husband in the toilet bowl, thought Lou, and she's lecturing me on sanity. "Look," he said, "I don't want to hear no more nonsense about trying to pin Floyd's murder on me."

She looked at him worshipfully. "I won't, Lou. As long as I know we're going to be together."

163

Gently, he led her out of the bathroom and across the room to the front door. "Of course we are, angel," he said soothingly. "Only we're gonna get out of San Francisco."

"Really, Lou?"

"Really. Now you bring all the letters I wrote to you, and the gorilla pictures we took, and meet—"

"What about the slides?"

"What sl—"

"You know, with the sailor suits and the peanut butter?"

"Forget those. Just meet me tomorrow night at the Oakland Ferry. You got that?"

"Anything you say, darling," said Georgia.

Lou opened the door. Bess's eyes widened as she saw Georgia.

"That's a good girl," said Lou. "Now grab yourself a cab."

"But I didn't show you the name," whined Bess.

"Not you," said Lou, annoyedly. "Her!" He turned toward Georgia. "Try to get a good night's sleep."

"You know I'd do anything for you, Lou," said Georgia.

Bess cleared her throat and spat on the floor.

"Oh, hello, Miss Duffy," said Georgia. With habits like that, she thought, no wonder Lou has never given her a tumble.

"Hello, Mrs. Merkle," said Bess. She smiled broadly. "I'm awfully sorry I couldn't be at the funeral."

Georgia nodded. "We'll all miss him."

"He was a delightful person," said Bess. "Hardworking but not overbearing, intelligent without being pedantic, perverted without being a deviate. A prince of low-life, you might say."

Georgia inhaled. "Floyd is in his final resting place now . . . or soon will be."

"That's nice," said Bess sympathetically. "May I ask where that is?"

"Well," said Georgia, hesitantly, "he, uh. . . ."

"He was buried at sea," interjected Lou. "It's a kind of delayed interment, a new process."

Bess nodded. Georgia touched Lou's hand for a brief instant, then walked off toward the stairs.

"All right," said Lou to Bess, "come on in."

"I can wait if there's more," said Bess.

Lou grabbed her arm and pulled her in, slamming the door after them. "Sit down!" he said.

Bess sat. "Who *were* all those women?"

"Well, Mrs. Merkle you knew. The other two were members of a volleyball team I'm coaching. Now let's hear what you've got."

"Vladimir Tserejemiwtz is—Ezra C. V. Mildew Dezire, Jr.!"

Lou took the paper out of her hand and looked at it. "Wait a minute. There are two T's in Tserejemiwtz, none in the name you came up with."

"Ah, said Bess, holding up an index finger. "That was the whole key. Some people spell the Czar of Russia, T-S-A-R. But in America, we spell it C-Z-A-R."

"Which accounts for the fact that a malted like Blubber got stuck," said Lou enthusiastically.

"Right!" said Bess. "But when you use the American spelling, you come up with. . . ."

"Ezra C. V. Mildew Dezire, Jr.," said Lou, slowly.

"The owner of the Golden Gate Bridge!"

Lou lit a match and touched it to the paper; he watched the smoke curl up the slowly expanding, blackening edge. "You did fine, angel," he said. "How'd you ever get the answer?"

"Oh, the usual," said Bess.

"Oral sex with an idiot in a sub-basement?"

Bess looked stunned. "But—but—"

Lou chuckled. "When you been in the business as

165

long as I have, you learn to follow your hunches," he said.

"That was some hunch."

"All right," said Lou. "Just forget you ever heard that name."

"You mean Wunga?"

"Wunga? Who's Wunga? I mean Ezra C. V. Mildew Dezire, Jr. Don't ever repeat it to anyone."

"Even if," said Bess, "they capture me and prevent me from sleeping for six days, and then beat me mercilessly and use electric shock on my genitalia and then throw me in a dark, damp dungeon full of starving rats?"

Lou shook his head slowly. "Baby," he said, "I'm really sorry. You tell, and that could mean your job here. *Finito. Caput.* Goodbye, forty-three dollars and twenty cents a week minus tax and Social Security. Goodbye, classy office, typewriter, and the prestige of working for a private investigator. You gotta make a choice."

"I won't tell, don't worry," said Bess.

The phone rang. Lou nodded for her to pick it up, as the fire on the paper spread to his shirt sleeve.

"Hello? Yes, he is. Who's calling, please? Just a minute."

Lou snuffed out his shirt. "I got a hunch that's my broker," he said. "I've spent twenty years going with these hunches."

Bess shook her head no.

"Not my broker," muttered Lou. "My kindergarten teacher?"

Bess shook her head again.

"My tailor? No . . . couldn't be. He died before I was born. My knife-sharpener?" His face dropped. "All right, fuck these hunches, who is it?"

"It's him," whispered Bess, "Ezra C. V. Mildew Dezire, Jr."

Lou shot her a pained look. "I told you not to repeat that name!" He shook his head and took the phone. "And there weren't even any rats," he said ruefully.

Then, into the receiver: "Hello . . . Yes. Yes, Mr. Dezire. No, the rats referred to another conversation I was having." He removed a pencil from his pocket, found a piece of paper, and scribbled on the arm of the couch. "Yes, I have the address. Ten o'clock tomorrow morning. Not at all. It's my pleasure, sir."

He hung up and punched his palm with his fist. "Eeeeeeyahooooo! Wheeeeeeeeeeee! Hunky dory! He wants to see me. The pieces are beginning to fit, angel." He leaned over and squeezed Bess's arm.

Bess moved closer to him.

"And I've got you to thank for it," said Lou.

Bess looked up at him longingly. "Go ahead, Lou, thank me. Thank me here. Now! You don't know how long I've waited for a good thank."

"Are you trying to tell me that . . ." Lou tried to keep the amusement from his voice.

Bess lowered her eyes. "Yes . . . I know I look like I've been around, but I've never been thanked in my life."

"But how about that business with the idiot?"

"Idiot-savant," corrected Bess, "and that was an unnatural act, not a thank. There's a world of difference."

"You sweet, silly kid," said Lou, "why haven't I ever noticed you before?"

He moved toward her and took her in his arms.

"I'm not wearing a girdle now," said Bess. "Could that be it?"

Before Lou could answer, there was a knock on the door. "Who is it?" he yelled, annoyed.

"Lady Edwina Morgan St. Paul," came a woman's voice.

167

Lou sighed. "It's crazy Mrs. Montenegro. Sorry, angel, I'm afraid I'll have to give you that thank some other time."

He released Bess, walked to the door and jerked it open. Mrs. Montenegro stood in the hall. She wore an English tweed suit, a hat with a banana and strip of bacon on top, and orange-framed glasses. "Thank you for seeing me, Mr. Peckinpaugh," she said.

Bess, on her way out, hurried past. "I *knew* there'd be one more. G'night, Lou."

"Good night, kid," said Lou. He turned back to Mrs. Montenegro. "You were saying. . . ."

"I was hoping you could help me find a Rumanian butler who used to work for me."

Lou smirked.

"Why are—?"

"It's the bacon on your hat," he said. "I've always been amused by bacon, I don't know why."

"Perhaps the curling. . . ."

"Perhaps. At any rate, you want me to find this butler for you."

"Yes. He used to be in my employ. His name is—"

"I *know* his name, Mrs. Montenegro."

The woman's shoulders slumped. Then, relaxing, she grinned. "What gave me away?"

"This time?"

"This time."

"Well," said Lou, "last night I just happened to be reading a book on abonormal behavior. You were on every page."

He slammed the door.

"You want my opinion?" said the cabbie. "We're gonna be drawed into the war."

"Oh, yeah," said Lou.

"No question. The krauts got France now, they got most of the rest of Europe, the Japs I don't trust for one second, there's no question. We'll be in it up over our ears."

"All right," said Lou. "I'm listening. What do we do?"

"My opinion?" said the cabbie. "We attack England."

"England?"

"Then we hit Canada and Mexico simultaneously."

"But these are our friends," said Lou. "Why attack our friends?"

"Simple," said the cabbie. "The Krauts are unstoppable, right? They got the Russkies and the Nips, and it's clear it's just a matter of time before they take Britain, right? I mean, pluck only gets you so far. So my idea is we conquer England before them, while the British are weak, and then we use Britain as a bargaining point. Maybe offer them half, if they make peace and leave us alone."

"But you can't trust them!" said Lou.

"That's where Canada and Mexico come in," said the cabbie, as they pulled onto the grounds of an enormous estate. "You show the Heinies they can't trust us either, that here we are turning on our best friends. It'll make them afraid of us, see. Make them think we're crazy."

"In your case," said Lou, "that won't take much."

They came to a huge iron gate that blocked the private road. Suddenly the gate swung open, permitting them to drive through and pull halfway around an enormous, semicircular driveway. They stopped in front of a graceful, white-pillared mansion.

"I think we're at the library," said Lou.

He got out, paid and tipped the cabbie, and then made his way up the stone portico until he reached the ornately carved, heavy oak front door. He looked around and wondered at the value of all this. How much money was invested here? A quarter-million? A

169

million? Ten million? It was vast beyond his wildest dreams. Imagine life's inequities, thought Lou. There were people in the world who were starving, and others who had million-dollar estates. He turned, and noticed the taxi had not left. The driver leaned out the window. "I was thinking," he called to Lou. "It also makes sense to attack Florida."

Lou pressed the doorbell. Chimes played the first eight notes of "America the Beautiful." After a moment, the door opened part way, and Lou found himself staring at the butler, a very tall man with an incredibly snobbish face and cold, calculating eyes. He looked Lou up and down as one might examine an insect.

"I'm Lou Peckinpaugh," said Lou, nervously. "I have an appointment with Mr. Dezire."

The butler stared at him and sneered. "Well, I suppose that's his business."

He opened the door farther and stepped aside. Lou entered, and as he did so, the butler snapped his fingers, indicating a floor mat. Hurriedly, Lou wiped his feet, doing an unusually thorough job. When he'd finished, the butler unceremoniously kicked the mat out the door. Lou glanced around. He stood on a highly polished marble floor in an immense entrance room. The ceiling was at least thirty feet high and from it hung two glittering chandeliers. A marble staircase led to an upper floor, and intricately woven tapestries adorned the walls.

"Do you want my hat?" Lou asked hesitantly. For the first time in his life, he had to admit, he was awed.

"I don't take hats," said the butler, patronizingly. He pressed a button on a small table, and a side door swung open. A large monkey scampered out and took the butler by the hand. Both of them looked at Lou. "*He* does," continued the butler.

"He does what?" said Lou.

170

"*He* takes hats."

"Oh. Right."

Lou gave the monkey his hat. The monkey put it on his head and returned to the room from which he'd come.

"I hope he washes his hair regularly," said Lou.

"Perhaps," said the butler, "he's wishing the same about you. And now, if you'll follow me, Mr. Pawkinpeck."

Lou grimaced as they walked across the entrance hall and came to a set of twenty-foot-high double doors. Lou waited.

"I don't open doors," said the butler.

"All right," said Lou, "where's the trained goat, or the door-opening monkey, or whatever?"

The butler merely looked straight ahead. A discerning observer might have detected the tiniest nasty grin on his lips. Actually, even a dull observer might've seen it. Eventually, his patience wearing as thin as the soles on his shoes, Lou shoved open the door.

"Wait in here, please," said the butler.

"Do you mind if I smoke?" asked Lou.

The butler pursed his lips together. "If it were *my* house, yes."

He closed the door, leaving Lou alone. Lou lit up a cigarette and looked for an ashtray. He was in a lush library, the walls lined with mahogany shelves housing rows and rows of impressively bound volumes. The collection was eclectic: a twenty-book set entitled *Man's Place in the Universe* stood next to a pocket edition of *Motorcycle Mamas*. On an end table Lou found a ceramic ashtray, hand-painted to look like a lily-of-the-valley. He quickly slipped it into his pocket. Near one shelf hung an oil painting of the Golden Gate Bridge, specially framed with distressed pecan and carefully illuminated by non-glare lamps. A large fireplace took up a rear wall.

171

"Glad to see a fresh face around here," said a voice. Lou whirled. Leaning languidly against the door frame was the most striking woman he had ever seen. She had long red hair that flowed over one eye and down her back; she wore black silk pants that clung to every contour of her body and a black silk shirt that erupted spectacularly at the chest. Diamond earrings dangled from her earlobes; she wore diamond bracelets on her wrists, diamond rings on nearly every finger. From the way they reflected the light, Lou knew this was the real stuff, no costume jewelry here. In her right hand, he saw a small box covered with buttons and lights.

"I'm Jezebel Dezire," said the woman huskily. "Accent on the Dezire."

"Lou Peckinpaugh," said Lou. "Accent on the peckin."

"Ezra just got up from his nap," said Jezebel. "I'll bring him in."

She pressed a button on the box she carried, and an old man, easily in his eighties, came tooling in on a wheelchair. Jezebel stopped him in the center of the room, then pressed another button that made the chair pivot forty-five degrees, so that it now faced Lou.

Lou took a step forward and extended his hand. "How do you do, sir."

Jezebel pressed another button and the old man's hand shot out to meet Lou's. Lou shook it, and then Jezebel made it retract.

"This gadget can make him do anything," she said. "Up to a point."

Lou looked down into his palm and saw a small, folded square of paper. Quickly, he closed his hand to conceal it. The old man looked at him with watery, pleading eyes.

"Your father here called last night," said Lou. "He said he needed my services."

172

"He's not my father," said Jezebel.

"Oh, well—"

"The old coot is my husband."

"Oh . . . I'm sorry," said Lou.

"You can imagine how I feel," said Jezebel.

She picked up a small bottle from the end table, opened it, and tapped until a pill came out. While she was thus engaged, Lou opened his palm and unfolded the square of paper inside. It was a message: "Don't trust her!" Jezebel crossed to the old man.

"It's time for your pill, Wrinkles. Open up."

The old man didn't move.

"He likes the cotton from the bottle better than the pills," said Jezebel to Lou.

"Good way to dry out if you drink too much water," said Lou.

Jezebel returned her attention to the old man. "I said, open up!"

There was still no movement.

Jezebel laughed menacingly. "Don't get cute with me!"

She took a step backwards, then pressed a remote control button. The old man's mouth snapped open. She threw the pill at his chin and missed.

"Oops," she said, bending to retrieve it. "See," she said to Lou, "like pool. Or Golf."

She threw the pill again, this time landing it in the old man's mouth. A push of a button, and his jaws slammed shut. A second push, and his mouth crushed the pill while his throat swallowed the pieces.

"That's better," said Jezebel. "You need your strength if you want to play hockey in bed tonight."

"Jesus," said Lou, shaking his head. "Jee-sus! That little box has some power."

"The best way I know to control a man," said Jezebel, "is with a powerful little box." She winked at Lou and blew exaggerated kisses in his direction.

The old man made a wheezing sound.

"Was that a wheeze or a rasp?" asked Lou.

"Look at his eyes," said Jezebel.

Lou looked. A murderous anger burned its way through the rheumy glaze. "I think it was a seethe," said Lou, feeling embarrassed.

Jezebel extended her hand seductively. "I'm so grateful you're going to help my husband, Mr. Peckinpaugh."

Lou took her hand in his own. It was soft and very warm, almost pulsating. "This is some nice hand you got here," he said admiringly. "This is one of the four or five top hands I've held."

Jezebel looked away demurely. "There's just so much I can do by myself."

"It takes two to tango," said Lou.

"There's strength in unity," said Jezebel.

"The more the merrier. Jesus, what a hand!"

Slowly, Jezebel slid from Lou's grasp. He looked down; in his palm he saw a small, folded square of paper. He turned sideways and opened it. Must be my day for notes, he thought. He read the message: "Don't trust him, either."

"We seem to have come full circle," he said.

Jezebel had walked around behind the old man. "It's chilly in here, don't you think?"

"Me?" said Lou.

Jezebel nodded.

"I'm fine," said Lou.

"I think my lammykins is cold," said Jezebel to the old man. "Wouldn't you like to sit near the nice, cozy fire, dear?"

A look of panic crossed the old man's eyes. Jezebel picked up the box from the table where she'd placed it.

"I don't think he's cold," said Lou.

"Of course he is," said Jezebel, brushing a strand of red hair from her eye. "Here we go."

She pressed a button, and the wheelchair began to move toward the huge, open fireplace.

"Is that wood you're burning?" asked Lou.

The chair rolled inexorably forward.

"Yes," said Jezebel, "but it will incinerate most anything."

The old man flashed past, his face a mask of pure terror. Jezebel smiled expectantly. She's really going to do it, thought Lou.

"That's no way to conserve energy," he said, rushing over to grab the box from Jezebel, just as the wheel of the chair touched the first brick of the fireplace. He pressed the button, and the chair came to an instant halt.

"Oh, thank you," said Jezebel casually. "It must've stuck, or something."

"I keep telling people," said Lou. "Most accidents happen right in your own home."

"This might've been a nasty one," said Jezebel. "My husband could've become a fine, white ash that"—she extended a palm, and placed her mouth at the edge of her hand—"I could've simply . . . blown away." She blew.

Lou looked back at the chair, stopped less than a foot from the fire. "Shouldn't we, uh . . . ?" He handed Jezebel back the remote control, and she pressed a button.

The chair spun around a hundred and eighty degrees. The old man was perspiring profusely, the water running in streams down his forehead. On his face was the most profound look of relief Lou had ever seen.

"I think we all need a little drinky," said Jezebel.

She walked to the corner of the room where there was a small bar. On the way, she brushed close to Lou; he felt the firm, yielding contours of her bosom against his chest.

"Sorry," she said.

"I'm not," said Lou.

She opened a bottle of bourbon and filled a glass halfway. She held it against her cleavage as she leaned on the bar. "What's your pleasure?" she said.

Lou inhaled deeply. "What you've got there looks very good."

Jezebel grinned. "Swell, but I thought you'd like a little drink first."

Lou glanced over at the old man. His features were contorted with rage; his nose had moved up almost to his eyes, and his ears were down near his chin. A teeny, tiny sound came from his throat. "Nnnn. Nnnnnn."

"Excuse me, sir," said Lou. "Are you trying to say something?"

"Nnnnn." Quaking. "Nnnnnn."

"I can't seem to hear you, sir."

"Forget it," said Jezebel. "It's just the wheelchair humming. Maybe his motor needs oiling."

Lou felt embarrassed, felt he ought to say something. After all, he was a guest in the old man's house, there by his invitation. He decided to attempt politeness. "Nnnnn" said Lou, pleasantly.

"Nnnnn," said the old man, the veins bulging in his neck and forehead.

This is no good, thought Lou. He's getting apoplectic.

"Maybe he has to take a crap," suggested Jezebel.

Lou tried another approach. He smiled and pointed at the painting of the Golden Gate Bridge. "I've, er— been over your bridge many times, sir."

"Nnnnn."

"You certainly have a wonderful location there, right over the water and everything."

"Nnnnn."

"You're making yourself a moron," said Jezebel. "Forget him. He gets cheerful later." She ran her

176

tongue slowly over her lips. "Now, would you like anything to . . . nibble on?"

"I—"

She rubbed her finger on the rim on the glass. She had long, tapered, red-polished nails.

"I—don't nibble on the job, thank you," said Lou. He noticed the old man seemed to relax a bit.

"Eating is good for you," said Jezebel. "Don't you ever eat, Mr. Peckinpaugh?"

Lou rubbed the back of his neck. "Yes. Yes, I love to eat. Most of the time I can't afford it, that's all."

Jezebel pursed her lips. "Well, there's lots of free meals around, if you know how to look."

Lou decided he couldn't take much more. "Just how did you happen to call *me*, Mrs. Dezire?"

"I picked it out of the phone book."

"Just like that? At random?"

"Mmm, maybe not at random, exactly."

"Then you knew about me, or heard of me?"

"I liked the sound of your name, Peck 'n' Paw. Know what I mean?"

Lou looked at the old man. "I think everyone knows what you mean."

The old man said, "Nnnnuhh."

"Oh," said Lou. "See? A new word. That's wonderful, sir."

"Nnnnuhh."

"You've got a nicely built house here, sir." And a terrifically built wife, thought Lou.

Jezebel walked over to a sofa and sensuously massaged the velvet.

I think I should tie myself up, thought Lou. Or down.

"Why don't you pull up a sofa and sit?" said Jezebel.

"Thank you," said Lou.

He sat down on a second sofa, this one upholstered in the softest red velvet he'd ever touched. He faced the old man. Jezebel came over and placed her delicious, ripe-peach behind on the sofa's back. Between the combination of this material and her ass, thought Lou, I believe I'm going to pass out. He inhaled her perfume, a tangy scent of orange blossoms and magnolias. He addressed the old man.

"You said on the phone, sir, you thought I could be of some help to you."

"That," said Jezebel, "depends on how 'helpful' you are. I suppose you give good service to your clients?"

"I try to satisfy," said Lou. He smiled weakly at the old man. "Sometimes I give bonuses."

"Coupons?" said Jezebel. "Is that it? You tear off a few coupons." She toyed with the hair at the back of his neck.

Lou's body began to tingle all over. I'm coming apart, he thought. Another few minutes, I'm gonna jump her. "Something like that," he said.

"Do you charge by the hour?" said Jezebel. "Or by the satisfaction?"

The old man squeezed the right side of his wheelchair then, and Lou could see the stringy muscles and tendons quivering in his arm. After five seconds, a piece of the wheelchair broke off.

"By the results," whispered Lou.

"Goody, goody," said Jezebel. She blew in his ear.

"That's one of the three things on earth that get me absolutely crazy and uncontrollable," said Lou.

"And the other two?" said Jezebel, not stopping.

"The second is a really good egg cream," said Lou. "And the third involves a case of soft margarine and a lot of rubber tubing—I'd rather not go into it."

Jezebel kept working on the ear.

Lou looked at the old man and smiled. "I, er, take it the old boy is pretty deaf."

"He hears everything we're saying," said Jezebel.

"Oh?" said Lou. "Really?" He kept up his phony smile.

"Really," said Jezebel. She was breathing heavily.

"How you doin' there, old-timer?" said Lou, waving.

"Forget him," said Jezebel. "Ignore him."

"Why?"

"Otherwise, he'll want to come everywhere with us."

Lou nodded. "Doesn't he mind . . . all this?"

Jezebel momentarily stopped her ear work. She smiled. "Drives him crazy."

"It drives him crazy," repeated Lou. "All right. Then why doesn't he say anything?"

Jezebel guffawed. "Are you crazy? He's only got five good minutes a day."

"Five good minutes?"

"In which he can speak. He's got to save it for dinner. Otherwise, he can't even ask for the salt."

Lou, his ear beginning to clear, and with it, his mind, said quickly, "Look, you're a very attractive woman, Mrs. Dezire, but—"

"Thank you."

"—but I'm here on business at your husband's request."

Jezebel walked around to the front of the sofa.

"Now," continued Lou, "why did he call me last night?"

Jezebel sprawled on the couch next to Lou. She put one foot on his lap. "He thinks I'm cheating on him," she said in a pussycat voice.

"I wonder why," said Lou.

"He wants you to find out who the man is." She put the other foot on his lap and began to work both heels back and forth. Oh no, thought Lou. He stood up abruptly and walked to the fireplace.

"Yeah, well, I got a strange feeling it's *me*," he said.

Jezebel sat up demurely. "Some of my jewelry is missing."

179

"Did you lose it?"

"Ezra thinks I gave it to my lover."

Lou nodded and looked at her sharply. "Did you give it to him?"

Jezebel's smile returned. "Everything but my jewelry." She wagged her head back and forth playfully.

The old man pounded the remaining good side of his chair with his fist. He stomped his feet. "Grrrrrunnnn!"

"Hey!" said Lou. "You hear that?"

"What?"

"He made another new sound. Grun. That's what he said. Grun."

"Oh, that's an old one," said Jezebel. "It means if he catches me, he'll chop the guy's nuts off and pour boiling oil between my legs."

"Very charming," said Lou. The old guy's just about apoplectic, he thought. Agitate him a little more and he could go right here.

"Listen," he said quietly. "Ixnay on the sexnay, otherwise he won't make it to dinner."

"More for us," said Jezebel.

"What kind of jewelry is missing?" asked Lou.

Jezebel shrugged. "Oh, nothing important."

"Like what?"

"Oh, just a few trinkets and burbles."

Lou narrowed his eyes and widened his nose. "Trinkets and what?"

"Burbles!"

"I'm sorry. . . ."

"You know . . . like burbles and bangles."

Lou nodded, and chuckled derisively. "The word you mean, Mrs. Dezire, is 'baubles.' "

"Yes, that's it," said Jezebel quickly. "Burbles."

"If you were American," continued Lou, "you would have known that."

"I am American," protested Jezebel. "I—" She began to sing. "Oh, say can you see, by—"

Lou shook his head.

"The Yankees," said Jezebel. "Teddy Roosevelt. Kansas. The Alamo." Her voice grew weaker. "Al Jolson. Boss Tweed. *The Lung Ranger*. The—"

"You see?" said Lou. "There it is again. *'The Lung Ranger.'* It was never a medical show, Mrs. Dezire."

Jezebel looked around frantically.

"You see," said Lou slowly, "the fact is, it's only Rumanians who pronounce the word 'burbles.'"

"And Latvians," said Jezebel sadly.

"No," said Lou. "A Latvian says 'bourbles.' You hear the difference?"

Jezebel nodded.

"But you are Rumanian," said Lou, "and that's why that word gave you trouble, Mrs. *Vladimir Tserijemiwtz!*"

Jezebel appeared about to faint. Then, suddenly, she snapped upright and turned to her husband.

"I tolt you ve vouldn't get away vith it."

"She tolt you," repeated Lou.

"I tolt you it vas a shtupid idea," said Jezebel.

"She tolt you it vas shtupid," echoed Lou.

"I tolt you I couldn't say 'burbles.'"

"She couldn't say 'baubles,'" said Lou. "Hey, how about 'pauper'? Can you say that?"

"Purper."

Lou smiled.

"You're pretty fast on your tiptoes, meester Pockinbush," said Jezebel.

Suddenly the old man tore the blanket off his lap. Underneath was his hand, pointing a large carrot at Lou. "But not quite fast enough," he said in a clear voice, motioning Lou to raise his hands.

XI

"Broccoli I wouldn't go near," said Lou, "but I'm not afraid of carrots."

The old man glanced down, then quickly replaced the carrot with a large black revolver that lay on his other knee. "I could kill you with either one," he said. "Now raise those hands."

Lou complied.

The old man smiled. "As you so cleverly deduced, I am, of course, Vladimir Tserimej—Tsemejem—." He shook his head. "It's been so long I can't pronounce it any more."

"Tserijemiwtz," filled in Lou.

"Tsank you."

"My pleasure."

."As you may have guessed," said the old man, "the Albanian eggs were stolen from my safe last night."

"Doesn't surprise me," said Lou.

"Also taken were the Persian cheese and two pieces of Danish pastry."

Lou grinned.

"I had an apple strudel made of pure platinum," said the old man softly. "The filling was gold cream."

"Cold cream?"

"Gold. A cream made of the finest pulverized gold, beaten till fluffy."

"I'll add it to my recipes," said Lou.

"At first," said the old man, "I suspected Blubber, Damascus, and Mrs. What's-her-name."

"Forget it,' said Lou. "It's a can of worms."

"Mrs. Acanofworms."

"I think we're gonna be here all night," said Lou.

"Permit me," said the old man, "to introduce my oversexed wife, the former Nadia Gladdia Poppenescu."

"Nice to meet you," said Lou to the former Jezebel.

"Anytime, anywhere," said Nadia.

"Very touching," said Vladimir, the former Old Man. "However, since you are the only one who can identify me, Mr. Chickenpoop, I—"

"Peckinpaugh," said Lou, the about-to-be-former private detective, "and other people know my whereabouts."

"Balonyeh," said Vladimir. "Is that how you say? Yes?"

"Baloney," said Lou.

"Yes. As you said. Ah, the speech here is, uh, is—"

"Baloney," said Nadia.

"No," said Vladimir, his eyes lighting up. "Is picturesque. Yes? Yes. I like."

"Very good," said Lou. "Want to try for baubles?"

Vladimir shook his head. "I'm sorry, but I must bring this meeting, and your life, to a close. Good-by-chik."

"So longski!" said Nadia.

"Listen," said Lou, loosening his collar. "Can the

184

Rumanian. Knocking me off isn't gonna find out diddley about who took your diamonds."

"Diddley?"

"It's an expression."

Vladimir laughed. "But I already know who took them."

Lou looked stunned. His mind felt empty.

"I had a partner," said Vladimir.

"A partner?" said Lou, blankly. "When?"

"That night in Paris in nineteen thirty-one. But he was much too greedy a man. He insisted on sharing the diamonds."

"Some people have severe character defects," said Lou.

"We worked it out amicably, though," said Vladimir. "I shot him."

Lou nodded. "I always heard you Rumanians were hotheads."

Vladimir shrugged and grinned slyly. "It's just the gypsy in our soul."

He moved his chair closer to Lou, keeping his revolver pointed directly at Lou's heart. So intense was his concentration that he failed to notice the tip of the silencer suddenly thrust through the satin draperies.

Vladimir went on. "Unfortunately, he did not die. I left him bleeding on the floor."

"You didn't kill him?"

"I didn't have time. People were coming. It was a mistake. If you want to do something badly enough, you *make* the time. I learned a lesson."

"And what finally happened?"

"He vowed he would get me one day. Those were his words, 'I vow one day I will get you.'"

"But so far, he hasn't."

"That was ten years ago,' said Vladimir. "He can't last much longer." He cocked the revolver and smiled. "But then again—"

185

"Wait," said Lou.

"—neither can you, I'm sorry to say. Goodbye, Mr. Pickleball!"

He raised his arm to fire, but before he could, the silencer from the drapes went "Thwp! Thwp!" and a bullet hole appeared almost magically in his forehead. Vladimir stiffened and became rigid, still sitting up, his outstretched arm remaining pointed at Lou.

"Behind the drapes!" said Nadia.

"What?" said Lou, reacting quickly.

"The gun!"

"Oh. Oh, yeah." Lou walked over and pulled open the drapes. Behind them, the French windows were open. A light breeze was blowing in from the southwest. Lou looked down. The floor was splashed with brownish red blood, but there was no sign of the killer.

"Quite a guy," said Lou. "He's been bleeding for ten years, and he's still fast as a rabbit."

"Can you tell anything?" said Nadia, her face still white from the shock, and from spending much time indoors.

Lou knelt and examined the blood. "He's anemic," he said, "which you might expect. He ought to take an iron supplement. His blood type is probably O. And—"

"How could you tell that?" asked Nadia. "Don't you need lab tests, or something?"

Lou nodded. "Well, a lot of people think that," he said, "but it's a little-known fact, see, that when you bleed heavily, you almost always bleed in the shape of your blood-type letter. Now you see that ring on the floor?"

Nadia nodded.

"That's why I say he's type O," explained Lou. "If you see an A on the floor, your man is probably type A."

186

Nadia looked at him. "I think you must really be cracked," she said.

"The ones you almost never get are the AB positives," said Lou. "They usually die before they can spell out what they are."

"Anything else?" asked Nadia impatiently.

"Yeah," said Lou. "Whoever he was, he had a lousy silencer. I mean, I could hear the thing clearly. So we got that to work on also."

"It's your move," said Nadia.

Lou thought a moment, then said, "All right, we have to check out a few things first." He walked across the library and opened the doors to the entrance hall. It was empty. "Hello?" he shouted.

There was no answer.

"Hello? Anyone there? Hey!" His voice echoed off the marble floors and stairs and the high ceiling. "Hello? Hey, butler! Hey, you around?"

After a moment, a side door opened and the butler emerged. He walked slowly over to Lou and looked at him down the full length of his nose. "Yes?"

"There's been a murder," said Lou. "Mr. Dezire's been shot and killed by an unknown assassin."

"Rotten luck," said the butler, his expression unchanged. "Fortunately, my job security is determined by my ability, not my background."

"I happen to be a private detective," said Lou, quickly flashing his wallet, "and I'd like to ask you some questions."

"That's a terrible-looking wallet," observed the butler.

"It doesn't get much use," said Lou. "Would you step inside the library, sir?"

"Why?"

"Because I—I just told you."

"I mean, why should I talk to you at all? You're not the police."

187

Lou smiled. "Ah, very true. However, my work has led me to form many close friendships with those on the force. If I were to suggest, for example, that you might be implicated here in some way, I'm certain they'd take that very seriously. They'd probably ask you down to the station, question you for six, seven hours at a time, maybe detain—"

"I see your point."

"If you cooperate, however, and you're in the clear," said Lou, "they won't spend more than five minutes—"

"I *see* your point!" said the butler. He headed toward the library. "Let's get this over with."

"Fine," said Lou graciously. "Oh, one more thing. Are there any other household staff members present? I'd like to question them, too."

"There is no one," said the butler. "It is the staff's day off, except for me. I work continuously. That is why Mr. Dezire always considered me more than staff. He often said, 'I never think of you as a butler.' That was when he was confusing me with Armand, the chauffeur."

"But you're the only other person in this house?" persisted Lou.

"Myself, and the monkey, who took your hat. Now, *there* is someone Mr. Dezire definitely thought of as staff."

"Ask the monkey to come in, please," said Lou authoritatively as he entered the library.

The butler shook his head, but did as he was told. A moment later, he and the monkey came in.

"Sit down, please," said Lou.

The butler and the monkey sat next to each other on the couch. Lou removed a small pad and a pencil from his pocket.

"Name?" he said to the butler.

"Edward."

"Edward what?"

"Edward is my last name. My first name is Edouard."

"Edouard Edward," repeated Lou, as he wrote on his pad. "And you, sir?" he asked, turning to the monkey.

"Cheech!" yelled the monkey, showing teeth with many cavities.

"Cheech," said Lou, as he wrote. "You both live here on a full time basis?"

The monkey screeched.

Lou turned to Edouard. "Mr. Edward, can you understand him? I'm having a bit of difficulty here."

"Yes," said Edouard, with much disgust. "He says 'yes' to your question, and that applies to me also."

Nadia, sitting on the other couch, was shaking her head. "You must be quite mad, Mr. Peckinpaugh, questioning an ape like this, as if he were human."

"A good detective uses every available source of information," said Lou, "plus some unavailable ones." He returned his attention to the butler. "Mr. Edward, how long have you worked for Mr. Dezire?"

"Three years," said Edouard.

"And you, Mr. Cheech?"

"Eeeeeeeeeeee ahhhh eeeeeeee."

"He says a year and a half," translated Edouard.

"Meeeeeeee ahhhh eeeeeeeneeeee."

"What'd he say?" asked Lou.

The butler looked disgusted. "He wants to know if there's a reward for useful information leading to the capture of the perpetrator."

"He's no fool," said Lou. "Tell him it's worth three bananas."

"Neeeeeee ahh eeeenah."

The butler nodded.

"Well?" said Lou.

"He said your offer is an insult. He wants five thousand dollars in small bills, unmarked."

"I'll think about it," said Lou. "All right, the sixty-four-dollar question. Did either of you hear or see anything different or unusual just before Mr. Dezire was shot?"

"You Americans are dangerous lunatics," said Nadia. "I am finally convinced."

"Apart from your own presence," said Edouard, "everything was completely normal. You were abnormal, and still are."

The monkey began jumping up and down and squawking loudly.

"What's up?" asked Lou.

"He says," translated Edouard, "he *smelled* a strange presence in the house."

"Me?" asked Lou.

"Neeeeeahh eeeeeoooahhh."

"A different stink from yours."

"What kind of stink?" asked Lou.

A simian grin crossed the monkey's face.

"I'll get the five grand for you if the info is good," said Lou.

"Eeeefaheeeee reeeeeeneeeee."

"He says," said Edouard, "it was the stink of a Frenchman."

Lou nodded wearily and then decided to call it quits. He shook hands with Edouard and the monkey.

"Tell him to stay in the area," he said to the butler. "The police may want to know some more, take his fingerprints maybe."

As they went out the door, Edouard said to the monkey, "Remember, you promised me a cut."

Nadia laughed. "Ludicrous!" she said. "A ridiculous, ludicrous farce."

"Why?" said Lou. "I got some information."

"And you call that reliable. I happen to know they were lying to you from the beginning. The monkey's name, for instance. It's not Cheech, it's Ira."

The phone rang. "I'll take that," Lou said. "It's for me."

"You're sure?"

"Yes. Get a blanket or something and cover your late husband."

She removed the lace shawl from the top of the piano and flipped it over the corpse. Lou picked up the phone.

"Yes? Yes, angel, I'm fine. No, I'm not dead. Everything went like clockwork. It was the word 'burbles' that tripped her up, just like we figured."

"You planned that?" said Nadia. "Bullshitsky!"

"What's that?" said Lou into the mouthpiece. "When? I'm on my way." He hung up.

"So?" said Nadia.

"If you're smart," said Lou, "you'll stay out of this mess. The police have nothing they can pin on you."

Nadia nodded. "Maybe when dis is all over, you can come back and tich me how to say 'burbles.' "

Lou winked. "You just keep your door unlocked."

"I'll do better dan dot."

"Oh yeah?"

"I'll keep a lamp chop lit in the window."

Lou opened the doors of the library and waved goodbye. "Lamp chop," he muttered as he left.

It was late afternoon by the time he got back to his office. Bess was waiting for him.

"Am I glad you're here," she said.

"Are you?"

"Yes! But what happened to your hat?"

Lou took off his hat and looked at it. It was all torn and chewed. "Someone monkeyed with it." He flipped the hat on the cabinet.

"I've been trying to get hold of Betty," said Bess. "She's not at the club or the apartment. Hoppy's hopping all over town looking for her. I'm worried, Lou."

"So am I, angel."

She wrinkled her nose. "You, uh. . . ."

191

"Oh yeah, yeah. I was interviewing a witness who wasn't too clean. Listen, I'm gonna grab forty winks. Just keep your eye on the front door." He entered his own office and slumped down in his chair.

In the corridor outside, a man in a long, dark coat staggered and nearly fell. He breathed heavily and stopped to support himself against a wall. As he rested, a small pool of blood formed about his feet. When he moved ahead, the pool coalesced in the shape of the letter O.

Lou moved from his chair to the mangled old leather sofa he'd found the year before in a vacant lot. He lay down heavily and began winking his eyes open and shut.

"Twenty-seven . . . twenty-eight . . . twenty-nine . . ."

The door opened, and Bess stuck her head in. "There's a man dying to see you, Lou."

"Thirty . . . thirty-one . . . thirty—"

"I mean," said Bess calmly, "a man who's dying wants to see you."

Lou sat up. "Then show him in fast."

Bess swiveled around. "Mr. Peckinpaugh will see you now, sir."

The man lurched in. His hat and upturned coat collar covered his face. In his hands was a bundle, to which he clung tenaciously. Suddenly his legs gave way. He fell limply on the sofa, his head lolling backwards.

"Is he—?" said Bess, her eyes wide.

"Jewish?" said Lou. "I don't know. When we find out his name, I'll have a clue."

"I meant, is he . . . dead?"

"Dead?" said Lou. "I don't know. When we find out his name, I'll have a clue."

The man twitched.

"He shoulda been dead ten years ago," said Lou. He leaned over the man and removed his hat. "Marcel," he said softly.

Marcel groaned.

"Sorry about this, Marcel. Where'd he plug you?"

Marcel shook his head feebly.

"Can you talk?" said Lou. "If you can't talk, say 'I can't talk now.' All right, where are you hit?"

"Marcel looked up at him. "It was so long ago, I forget." He licked his lips.

"Get him a drink," Lou said to Bess.

"A nice Chablis, 'thirty-six, would be fine," said Marcel.

Bess nodded and rushed from the room.

Lou opened the buttons on Marcel's coat. "Are you comfortable?" he asked.

"Well," said Marcel, "I have some savings, a few municipal bonds, some short-term paper, some—"

"No, I meant here, on the sofa."

"I've slumped on better," said Marcel.

Lou looked down at him. A red stain was spreading quickly on the right side of his shirt, extending from the chest to the underarm and down the side. Lou winced. "Jeeesus! I think you'll have to miss a few days' work."

"Please, *monsieur*," said Marcel. "Refrain from zee jokes now, yes? This is not a happy time for me. I am down to only two unstained shirts."

"Anyone else would've died in two days from a wound like that," said Lou.

Marcel stiffened with pride, and also with pain. It is surprising, Lou thought, how many things can make a man stiffen.

"How did you stay alive for ten years?" he asked.

Marcel shrugged. "I cut out all salt and spicy dishes. But I'm afraid this is it, my friend."

Lou was touched. "Thanks for this afternoon."

Marcel waved nonchalantly.

"You already had the diamonds," said Lou. "Why did you stop Vladimir from plugging me?"

Marcel chuckled mirthlessly. A small gurgle of blood

193

began to come up in his throat. "It's true," he said. "I have the diamonds. But *you* had DuChard's papers." He tried to sit up. "You *do* have them?"

"You sound like you're gargling," said Lou. "Something get caught in your pipe?"

"Nothing important," whispered Marcel, lying back. "The papers, *monsieur?*"

"They'll be here any minute."

"I can't hang around much longer," gasped Marcel. "I have an appointment with zee grim reaper."

"Don't worry," said Lou. "He'll wait. His office is always crowded."

"Please—"

"Sit back and relax," said Lou. "Try to enjoy your last few minutes alive."

Marcel's face went slack.

"There's one thing I don't understand," said Lou. "You knew Tserijemiwtz was here in Frisco all these years." He lit a Camel and held it to Marcel's lips.

"You have anything milder?" choked Marcel.

"Sorry," said Lou.

Marcel took a drag.

"Now," continued Lou, "after double-crossing you like that in Paris, why didn't you kill him long ago?"

Marcel gave a watery chuckle. "My revenge was sweeter."

"Really. In what—"

"How would you like to be married to a tootsie like that, and not be able to get out of your wheelchair?"

Lou nodded and gave Marcel another drag on the cigarette. "Did you kill Floyd Merkle?"

"No."

"Can you prove that?"

"Yes. I was at home, bleeding on the carpet."

"But you've been bleeding for ten years. How do we know you were home on that particular night? You could have been bleeding anywhere."

"That night, the dry cleaners came over. They rolled up the carpet and took it back with them."

"You have their name and address?" asked Lou, whipping out a piece of paper and a small pencil.

Marcel gave him the information, and Lou let him take another drag on the Camel.

"Do I have to keep doing this?" asked Marcel. "I don't smoke."

"You don't?"

"I've heard it's dangerous for your health. I'm afraid one day it will kill me."

"It'll have to wait in line," said Lou. He put out the cigarette.

Suddenly, the door opened, and in flew Betty, breathless and perspiring. She was wearing her beret and trench coat.

"Don't get up, boys," she said.

Lou ran over to her. "You made it. Good girl!"

She tilted her head pixieishly. "If I was, I never would have gotten the papers."

XII

Lou took a deep breath; Marcel, two shallow ones. "You mean," said Lou, "that you and that pig Schlissel—?"

"*You* sent me there," said Betty.

Lou hung his head. Then he hung his arms and legs.

"It was terrible, Lou."

"Don't tell me what he did."

"He made me play war."

"Whore?"

"War. W—A—R."

"I dont want to hear about it. Did he tie you up and pretend you were his prisoner?"

"He was a Shtuka dive bomber and I was Poland."

Lou put a hand over his eyes. "*Forget it*, I said! Did

he strip you naked, and spread-eagle you on the floor so that you were helpless and exposed?"

"I had to pretend I was asleep," said Betty.

"That's sick."

"And then, in the middle of the night, I heard these great big bombers overhead. . . ."

Lou walked across the room. "*Why do you dames love to tell me these things?* They're degenerate, you hear? Perverted. Did he whip you with leather riding crops, and cover your heaving love nest with butterscotch pudding, and then get down on all fours and—?"

"I didn't have any heaving love nest," said Betty angrily.

"All right, forget that. What about the pud—All right, forget that, too. Just keep your filthy stories to yourself from now on."

"I'll try my best," said Betty.

"Now hand over the papers," said Lou, "because Marcel's about to check out."

"Death," said Marcel gently, "is merely nature's way of saying, 'slow down.' "

"He's been listening to too many commercials," said Lou. He held out his hand. "Okay, the papers. . . ."

Betty paused. "I don't have them."

"What?"

"I don't have them."

Lou shook his head. "I can't believe I heard what I heard."

"Perhaps," said Betty, "You heard what you can't believe, yes?"

Lou shot her a look of disgust. Then he shot her looks of pity, surprise, and nausea.

"When I left Schlissel's place, a car pulled up and someone grabbed me," Betty said.

"Was the someone in the car, or did he just happen to be on the street when the car pulled up?"

"In the car."

"Did you see who it was?"

"Yes. It was the punk kid who works for Blubber."

Lou punched the sofa with his fist. "Damn! I warned you about him! Didn't I warn you about him?"

"I don't think so."

"Well, watch out for him, then. He's crazy and dangerous, totally psychotic. I think he laughs when he's alone."

"He drove me out to the country on an old, deserted road."

Here we go again, thought Lou.

"Then he made me get out of the car," Betty said.

"I don't want to hear it!"

"He put on the car radio and made me dance the carioca."

Lou turned to Marcel. "They *know* it gets to me! That's why they all torture me like this!"

"I won't tell you how many times he raped me," said Betty.

"Don't tell me," said Lou. He shook his head. "Was it more than seven?"

"No."

"More than four?"

Betty shook her head no.

"Twice?"

"He never touched me. He said he's sick of men, women, and animals, and the only thing that arouses him are certain trees and small bushes. He mumbled something about an evergreen in front of a certain hotel. Said he was heartbroken because it threw him over for a young rhododendron."

"Somehow," said Lou, "I don''t quite believe you."

"It's true," swore Betty. "He says he's been sucking cholorphyll candies four or five times a day. He told me he's been spending more and more time in the sun."

"Enough!" said a phlegm-filled voice.

Lou whipped around.

199

Marcel had pulled a revolver from the folds of his coat and was aiming it at him shakily. "No papers, no diamonds! That was our deal, *monsieur*." Painfully, he got to his feet.

"No tickee, no shirtee," Lou agreed.

"The race goes to the swift," said Betty.

"You always miss the point," said Lou. "Hold it, maybe the phone will ring."

The phone rang.

"Maybe that's Blubber," said Lou. "Maybe we can still make a deal."

"Maybe!" mimicked Marcel. "Maybe this, maybe that. Maybes are cheap. Maybe the phone won't ring."

"But it just did," pointed out Betty.

"That's only one out of three," said Marcel.

Lou picked up the receiver. "Hello? Yes?" He nodded. "Yes, I was expecting your call." He smiled at Marcel.

"That's still only two out of three," said the dying Frenchman.

"I have the goods with me now," said Lou into the phone. "Shall we say my place in thirty minutes?" He paused. "I already said it. Now you." Lou listened, and then spoke. "And make sure the punk kid is there, I got a score to settle with him."

Betty looked pained.

"I heard all about the carioca," continued Lou. "And the what? He what? I don't want to know about it. I'm hanging up. I'm not listening!" He slammed down the phone.

He looked at Betty intently. "You didn't tell me about the beer barrel polka."

"I . . . couldn't bear it," she said softly. "Even to talk about it is to re-live the terrible shame and humiliation. There are certain depths of degradation that no human being—"

"All right, all right," said Lou. He turned to Marcel. "I need the goods, Marcel."

Marcel said nothing.

"You'll just have to trust me," continued Lou. "There comes a time in every man's life when finally he must place his fate in another's hands."

Marcel's face remained stony.

"You have my word as a licensed private detective," said Lou. "DuChard will be on that nine o'clock ferry with the papers in his hands." He reached for the bundle that Marcel still clutched tightly.

Marcel's expression was expressionless.

"Don't be stubborn, you crazy Frenchman!" yelled Lou in exasperation. "Time is on their side!"

"I don't think he's stubborn," said Betty. "I think he's dead."

"I think he's stubborn," said Lou.

"Dead," said Betty, flatly.

"Stubborn."

"Dead."

Lou looked at him closely. Marcel remained standing, his arms wrapped tightly around his bundle. Lou snapped his fingers in front of Marcel's lifeless eyes. There was no movement. Lou stuck his finger *in* Marcel's eye and poked around. There was no reaction.

"He's *very* stubborn," said Lou.

"I think you're projecting," said Betty. "Remember his last words? 'That's still only two out of three.' It might be a prophetic statement."

"All right," said Lou. "All right, I give. Just *once* on this case I'd like to see a man die regular."

He thought about the events of the last three days. Marcel had proved to be the link between what had seemed like separate sets of events.

Just then, Bess rushed in breathless, with a glass of white wine. She was dressed in a hat and coat. "I ran all the way," she gasped. "I hope I didn't spill any."

Lou ignored her. He reached over and tugged on the package in Marcel's arms. The Frenchman, maintaining a death grip, would not let go.

"You see?" said Lou. "I told you he was stubborn." He addressed himself to the corpse. "Will you be reasonable, now?"

The corpse maintained a discreet silence.

Lou pulled ferociously on the package, dislodged it, and headed for the door. "You should drop dead!" he said spitefully to the corpse. He grabbed a new hat from an end table and spoke rapidly to Bess.

"Call Lieutenant DiMaggio. Tell him where I'll be, but not to make a move until he gets my signal." He looked at her tenderly. "This may be the wrap-up, angel."

"And the kiss-off to me, is that it?" interjected Betty.

"I don't know," said Lou thoughtfully. "Tell me nothing happened."

"Is that what you want to hear?"

"Tell me. Even if you lie, I'll believe you. You can cross your fingers behind your back."

"Nothing happened," said Betty.

"Jesus," said Lou, disgusted. "It sounds worse than before." He stormed out of the office and slammed the door behind him.

I can't stand people who lie with a straight face, he thought. You can't tell if they're fooling or not. Liars should twist their features, or else wear wax lips, or some other tip-off to their behavior.

Inside the office, Bess looked wistfully at the closed door.

"I see you're looking wistful," said Betty. "You love him, too, don't you, kid?"

Bess shrugged. "He doesn't even know I'm alive. To him, I'm a number of a payroll. Sometimes he even forgets the number, although I'm the only employee. I guess I'll just have to 'thank' myself."

Both women felt morose.

The four of them waited in Lou's apartment.

Blubber sat on an armchair, part of him overlapping the sides and beginning to ooze down toward the floor. Damascus relaxed on the bed, leaving a body-shaped oil stain where he reclined. Mrs. Montenegro smoked nervously in the archway of the door. The Follower rested his gun carefully on the window ledge, squinting as he aimed it at the figure getting out of a cab below.

"No!" said Blubber sharply.

"Gotta end him," said the Follower.

"Not yet," said Blubber.

Reluctantly, the Follower backed away from the window.

"I say we kill him the minute he walks in the door with the bundle," said Damascus.

Blubber frowned. "You would like that, wouldn't you, you greasy imbecile?"

Damascus sat up. "We can put him in that chair and you can sit on him, you fat water buffalo." He giggled. The sound was like a car with worn brakes making an emergency stop. The others looked at him sternly.

"I'm having it fixed next week," he offered.

Mrs. Montenegro held up a hand. "Someone's coming up the stairs!"

"You know what to do," said Blubber calmly. "The minute you see the package in his hands, give him two additional eyeballs."

"Make it messy," giggled Damascus. "I love it when it's messy."

The doorknob turned, and the Follower raised his gun. In his mind, he pictured fragments of bone, hair, and blood being blown away like pieces of a mask. The image gave him great pleasure.

The door opened.

There, with a bundle in his hand, stood the cabbie. "I was told to deliver this to Mr. Peckinpaugh."

Before any of the four in the room could react, another voice came from behind them. "I'll take that, son."

The four spun around. Climbing in through the window was Lou, gun in hand, pointed steadily at the center of the Follower's face.

"One wrong move," he said, "and I'll blow your nose. Keep your hands up, everyone!"

The four raised their hands. Lou came forward and took up a position near the door, his back to the cabbie.

"Okay, driver, put the package on the table along with my change."

The cabbie placed the bundle on the table, and then took a quarter, three nickels, and a dime out of the coin-counter at his waist.

"Okay," said Lou. "Thanks. And keep a dime for yourself."

"A dime? After letting you climb on my back so you could reach the fire escape?"

"Listen," said Lou, "that's more than I've made on this case."

The cabbie muttered under his breath, "That's the last fare I let stand on my back!" He stomped angrily out the door.

Damascus squealed at the Follower. "Shoot him! What are you waiting for, you idiot? Use your gun!"

The Follower's eyes were crazed. "He'll . . . he'll kill me first."

"So?" said Damascus. "Who cares? I never liked you anyway."

"I need time to mull this over," said the Follower.

"Swell bunch of pals you got, sonny," said Lou. "All right, no time for mulling now. Mulling season is over. Throw your bed on the gun."

For an instant, no one spoke. Then Mrs. Montenegro said softly, "Gun on the bed."

"What?" said Lou.

"Gun on the bed," repeated Mrs. Montenegro. "You said, 'Throw your bed on the gun.'"

"Big deal," said Lou. "That's only the first mistake I made on this case. That's not bad, considering how complicated it is." He looked back at the Follower, who still held his revolver. "Go on," he said menacingly. "Throw it!"

The Follower tossed his gun on the mattress. Lou moved closer to him.

"Feel a little naked now, punk?"

"Not me," said the Follower.

"Now," said Lou, "we'll see how tough you are. Like to slap women around, don't you?"

The Follower's eyes lit up. "Not me."

"Well, let's find out how *you* like a little of the same," continued Lou. "Slap yourself in the face."

The Follower looked around at the others, but they averted their eyes. "Not me," he said.

"It's either that," said Lou, "or I use the business end of the gun."

"Use the pleasure end," suggested the Follower.

"Now slap yourself!" said Lou.

The Follower, embarrassed, smacked himself medium-hard across the face. A hand-shaped red blotch appeared on his cheek.

"You call that a slap?" said Lou. "That's a love tap! Now give it to yourself good. *Go on!*"

The Follower raised his arm again. The sound of his open hand striking his face cracked through the room. His cheek grew beet-red. Actually, thought the Follower, it doesn't feel that bad.

205

"Harder!" said Lou.

The Follower slapped himself harder. The sound was like a gunshot. Actually, thought the Follower, it feels good.

"Harder!" shouted Lou.

The Follower let go a tremendous blow to his jaw. A spot under his eye began to bleed. Actually, it feels fantastic, he thought. Excitement filled him. It was almost . . . sexual in nature.

"Harder!" bellowed Lou.

The Follower thought: Here is a thrill I can have any time for the rest of my life. And it is so harmless and wholesome. He wound up, and, using every muscle in his arm and back, belted himself with all his strength just under the cheekbone. The force of the blow sent him sprawling backward over the top of the chair and onto the floor. He lay there, floating in sweet unconsciousness.

Lou took out a handkerchief and wiped his forehead. "Anyone else want more of the same?"

No one took up the offer. After a moment, Blubber chuckled. "By gad, sir, you're a most extraordinary man. However, if you've had your fill of vengeance, perhaps we can get down to the important business of 'cracking eggs.' " He rose, and headed for the table.

"Not so fast, Chubbikens!" said Lou. "There's the little matter of DuChard's lease and liquor license."

Blubber smiled condescendingly. "By all means." He took a large white envelope from his inside pocket and extended it to Lou.

"Give it to the girl," said Lou.

Blubber shrugged. "As you wish." He turned to the woman. "Here you are, Miss Shearer."

"Who?" said Lou.

"Norma Shearer," said Mrs. Montenegro. "You told me to change it."

She crossed the room and took the envelope from Blubber.

"All right," said Lou, "give it here."

She handed the envelope to Lou. "You do care for me, don't you, Lou?"

Lou snorted demurely. "More than most women I've ever met. In fact, you *are* the most woman I've ever met."

"Oh, God, baby, if—"

"Now get back there with your pals."

Mrs. Montenegro looked hurt, but moved back with the others. Lou opened the envelope and examined the contents. "Everything seems to be in order." He put the envelope into his breast pocket and smiled.

"You . . . find this amusing?" said Blubber.

"Barrel of laughs," said Lou. He sat down on the bed and motioned with his gun. "Okay, folks, the bundle is all yours."

Blubber looked quickly at Damascus, who glanced at Montenegro. The play went six to four to three, if you're scoring. Feverish excitement lent an eerie glow to their eyes. Slowly, they gathered around the table on which the bundle lay. Damascus wiped some oil from where it floated atop his perspiration. Montenegro wet her lips furiously. Blubber breathed stertorously.

"Sixteen years," said the fat man. "A quarter of a lifetime I've waited for this moment." He bent and kissed the bundle.

"I'll be able to buy anything I ever wanted and never had," said Damascus. "Ceramic shoehorns . . . friends . . . a mother."

"I want to be young forever," said Mrs. Montenegro. "And money can make you young and fresh and beautiful. Hurry! Open the package quickly, I want to look good *tonight!*"

Blubber grabbed the package and tried to undo the

207

string. He fumbled with it, his perspiring hands sliding on the waxed cord.

"You and your fat fingers!" said Damascus. "Let me do it!"

He tore feverishly at the package, but made little headway. After almost two minutes of struggling, he began to cry.

"Bite the string off, you idiot!" screamed Mrs. Montenegro. "Chew it! Eat it! Lick it off! Anything!"

The three of them (the Follower was still unconscious on the floor) tore into the package, as Lou watched with an amused smile. Finally, most of the string came off, and most of the newspaper wrapping, as well. Blubber held up an exquisitely gold-trimmed box shaped exactly like an ordinary egg container but clad with elegant crushed velvet. Damascus ran his hand sensuously over the surface.

"Open it!" he whispered. "Open it, quick, before the stores close!"

Blubber placed the box back on the table, undid the tiny gold clasp, and flipped up the cover. There, in separate compartments, rested twelve perfect, large-sized eggs, each nestled in a velvet holder. Blubber picked up one of the eggs, an unbroken, gleaming white shell.

"The treasure of Tibet!" he said. "One twelfth of all the wealth of ancient China."

"The diamonds!" said Damascus urgently. "I want to see the diamonds!"

They held their breaths as Blubber gently cracked the egg against a heavy metal ashtray that Lou had stolen from somewhere. A slight fissure appeared in the ashtray, and then in the egg.

"Easy!" said Damascus. "Easy!"

Blubber struck the egg again, and the crack widened. Again, and dozens of branching fractures appeared. He dug his pudgy fingers into the narrow crevices and pried apart the shell. A chirping sound startled them all.

The newborn chick fluttered weakly on the table as three gasps came simultaneously. A look of utter despair circulated from one person to the next like a telegram. No one could muster any speech. After a full minute, Blubber recovered sufficiently to extract a second egg.

"Always one bad egg in the bunch," he said, as he struck the second one against the ashtray. Again, he pried it apart, and again a newborn chick struggled to open its wings as it fell to the table.

"Shiiiit!" screamed Damascus.

He seized another egg and smashed it on the back of a chair. The chick that appeared was covered with pieces of shell.

They stopped at the seventh egg. Chirping and peeping filled the room. Squirming, turning, wriggling balls of feathery yellow covered the table.

"Chickees?" said Damascus tearfully. "Sixteen years I wasted on little chickees?" He turned to Blubber. "It's all *your* fault! Take them! They're all your chickees, you stupid, rotten, big, fat mother hen!"

He began to flail at the big man, his blows bouncing harmlessly off the thick layers of suet. Blubber, deep in his own grief, swatted once in a lazy arc, catching Damascus just below the ear and sending him sprawling over a chair.

"We've been duped," said the fat man sadly. "Tricked! The Polish gypsies' revenge."

Lou, who had been watching the spectacle calmly, now spoke up. "Sorry, folks, but I'm sending you over." He raised his voice and turned to the front door. "Come on in, boys!"

The door burst open, and three detectives plus two uniformed patrolmen tripped into the room.

"They're all yours, Frank," said Lou.

Lieutenant DiMaggio nodded.

Blubber straightened up. "And what is the charge, may I ask?"

"Yes," said Lou. "You may ask."

"The murder of Floyd Merkle," said DiMaggio, "plus five unimportant people."

Lou shook his head. "Sorry, Frank, but nobody here killed nobody. The most you got on them is a chicken-stealing charge."

"Plus premature hatching," said DiMaggio. "Lucky these chicks lived, or we coulda got them on illegal fowl abortion." He paused. "Then who *did* kill Merkle and the others?"

Lou shook his head. "All in due time, Frank."

"Listen," said DiMaggio, "If you know, I wanna know. Do you know?"

"I dont know . . . if I know."

"Listen, flatfoot—"

"All in due time," repeated Lou. And then, raising his voice, "Now get 'em outta here!"

The uniformed officers began herding Blubber, Damascus, and the Follower (who had just awakened) out the door.

Blubber turned to Lou. "My hat's off to you, sir. It was a pleasure doing business with a gentleman."

"Wish I could say the same," said Lou.

"Come on, ya fat cow," said one of the cops.

"You're an astounding man, Mr. Peckinpaugh," said Blubber, "but also, unfortunately, a pain in the ass."

"Thank you," said Lou.

Damascus tapped Blubber on the shoulder. "I don't mind, really, as long as we can be together."

"The only way we'll be together," said the fat man, "is if you bathe every fifteen minutes in concentrated mouthwash."

Damascus smiled. "I never really had a best friend. Most people were just interested in my looks."

"The only people interested in your looks must have been zoologists," said Blubber, as the two went out the door.

The Follower paused for a moment in front of Lou. "Lousy shamus!"

Lou ducked, just as the boy spat at him. Luckily, the Follower was untrained in spitting, and so most of the salivia simply ran down his chin and onto his shirt. He was still wiping his coat when the policeman pulled him through the doorway.

"What about Miss What's-her-name here?" said DiMaggio.

"Just drop her off at the Lost-and-Found," said Lou. "Someone'll pick her up."

"But, Lou," said Mrs. Montenegro, "I thought you and I . . ."

"Were what?" said Lou.

"Well, that we . . ."

"Could make beautiful music together? Sorry, I don't play. Were two of a kind? No, you're not even one of a kind. Had an understanding? I guess I didn't understand. Were meant—"

"Shut up, already," said DiMaggio.

Lou snapped out of it. "Sorry, beautiful."

"Don't call me beautiful," said DiMaggio.

"Look," said Lou, "I've got a date in twenty minutes at the Oakland Ferry." He ran into the bathroom, glanced at the clock, and dashed out again. "And this time I'm gonna keep it."

"Who's the lucky girl?" asked Mrs. Montenegro.

"You really want to know?"

"I can't help myself," said Mrs. Montenegro. "It's a compulsion I have—to always dig up the worst. I can't let sleeping dogs relax."

"She's . . . Marlene DuChard," said Lou.

Mrs. Montenegro slapped herself in the forehead.

211

"Oh, God, why didn't I think of that name? What a wonderful name! I could—"

"Look, it's more than the name."

"Marlene, Marlene, Marlene DuChard. Oh, gimme another chance, Lou."

"What?"

"Oh, Lou, please, it's me—Marlene! Lou—"

The cops dragged her out.

XIII

The ferry horn reverberated through the damp, foggy mist that rolled in from the blackness of the bay. It was just before nine o'clock, and already the night was chilled. Paul and Marlene huddled in the small, open shed on the pier as the last stragglers boarded the ferry. A single bare bulb lit the area. Paul checked his watch.

"Two minutes to nine."

"Oh, *merde!*" said Marlene, shivering.

"You know," said Paul, "I am a brave man, darling, but right now I feel the shit rising like a tide inside my pants."

"Be brave, *ma chérie*," said Marlene. "Maintain zee tight asshole, as the vulgar Americans say. He'll be here, Paul. He promised me."

Paul looked at her. "You—you went to his apartment that night, didn't you?" he said sadly.

"Who, me?"

Paul nodded.

"Yes . . . I'm sorry, Paul. How long have you known that Lou and I were lovers?"

"I didn't know," said Paul, gnashing his teeth, "until you told me just now. I thought you went there looking for me."

"Yes," said Marlene quickly. "That is why I went there. I made up the part about us being lovers because I know you don't like me looking for you." She turned away, the better to muffle and hide her laugh.

"What is that sound, darling?" asked Paul.

"I sneezed, *ma chérie,* that is all. My old ferry boat allergy, probably. I should have taken the shots."

Paul looked again at his watch. "One minute to go."

The roadster tore up the old country road, leaving clouds of loose dust in its wake. Colonel Schlissel sat up front in order to properly terrorize the driver, while the remaining two Germans occupied the rear.

Schlissel stared at his watch. "Ve can shtill make it if you hurry. Schnell! *Schnell!*"

One of the Germans in the back leaned forward. "Yes, sir?"

Schlissel inhaled. "I vass not talking to you, Schnell. I vass saying 'faster' to him in German. You speak German, chowderhead?"

"Yess, my Colonel," came the snappy answer.

"You understand now ze intent of ze command?"

"I understand, my Colonel."

"Zen sit back und shut your shtupid German mouth, you shvine!" screamed Schlissel.

The German snapped back.

"Four minutes to nine," said Schlissel. "Schnell!"

The German leaned forward. "Yes, sir?"

Schlissel clapped a hand to his forehead. "Ziss is vy ve vill lose ze war. Ziss, right here in ziss car. You understand zat, Schnell?"

"Yes, sir."

"Vy vill ve lose ze war?"

"Because I leaned forvard ven you called Schnell," said the German dutifully.

"English!" shrieked Schlissel. "Ve speak only English from now on! No more German!"

"Yes, sir."

"Sit back!"

"Yes, sir."

"Ve'll never make it," said Schlissel, panicky. "Qvicker! Qvicker!"

The other German leaned forward. "Yes, sir?"

"Not you, Qvicker! Forget it! It's a vaste of time!"

He looked sullenly out the side of the car. After a moment, he pounded the seat and began to whimper.

The warning bell from the ferry rang three times.

"They're leaving!" said Paul, biting his nails. "They're leaving without us!"

"That's only the first warning," said Marlene. "You must try to calm yourself, Paul."

Paul nodded and took a deep breath. "I'm sorry. I'm really wonderful in a war. I only get nervous when I'm late for things, or if I have to meet a new person."

"I know, darling," said Marlene.

"How do you know so much about ferries, anyway?"

"Oh, instinct, I guess. Also, I once read six books about them."

Just then a car pulled onto the pier and came to a screeching halt. The door opened and someone got out. Marlene and Paul strained to see, temporarily blinded by the headlights and the thick fog.

"The fog!" said Paul. "It's as thick as a—"

"As the jawbone of an ass," said Marlene.

"As the thighbone of a stegosaurus," came an answering voice.

And she knew immediately it was Lou, even before he came striding out of the night. Her features softened; her face suffused with love. For a moment, she imagined she heard a symphony orchestra.

"Sorry I'm late," said Lou, entering the shed. "I had some odds and ends to clean up."

"It's quite all right," said Paul. "Marlene got a little hysterical, but I calmed her down." He smiled at her and patted the top of her head.

"My hair!" she said.

"Sorry," said Paul. "I'd forgotten about the permanent."

"You have zee papers?" said Marlene to Lou.

He tapped his breast pocket. "I said I'd keep my word."

Tears formed in Marlene's eyes. Strangely, one even formed in her ear. "And I shall keep mine," she said.

"How can I ever repay you, *monsieur?*" asked Paul. "There's no point in me counting the ways. I have so little—what is there I can possibly give you in return?"

"How about your wife?" Lou said.

"No,". said Paul, considering. "She has nothing, either."

The ferry bells rang again.

"Second warning," said Marlene. "I remember that from *Why Is the Ferry Our Friend?*"

"Remarkable," said Paul.

Marlene turned to him. "Paul, there's something I think I should tell you."

"Can't you tell me on the boat, darling?"

"Maybe you two want to be alone," suggested Lou.

"No," said Marlene. "This is something that concerns us all. Paul, the last thing in this world I want to do is hurt you. No man has ever been kinder or more generous than you've been with me. But Louis is the only man I ever loved. I can't go with you, Paul. I'm going off with Louis. Now, tonight, forever.

Paul looked stunned. His knees began to buckle. "I feel," he said, "as if I have been hit by a board. You mean—I'm not getting the papers?"

Marlene's eyes widened. "Yes, you're getting the papers. You're just not getting *me*."

"But I *am* getting the papers?"

"I *said* you were."

Paul let out a breath. "Oh, my God! Oh, thank goodness! You know, you scared the life out of me."

"But, Paul, you—"

"I thought I wasn't getting the papers."

"—don't seem to understand. You're not getting me. I'm out. You and me—it's over. Gone with the—I dunno—tide."

"But the papers are mine."

Marlene looked hurt. "They seem to mean more to you than I do," she said quietly.

"Certainly not," said Paul. "But you have Louis. I think it's only right that I get the papers. What's sauce for the goose is sauce for the gander, as they say in the provinces. Fair is fair."

"Look," said Lou, "I don't want to be the cause of a family quarrel." He turned to Marlene. "Why don't you go with him and we can talk this out over dinner one night."

"I'm *not* going with him!" she said angrily. "I'm going with you. I just want you to know he's crazy about me. He's just being noble."

"No, I'm not," said Paul.

"I don't want to discuss it any more," said Marlene. "Just give him his *goddam papers!*" she yelled at Lou.

The bell on the ferry sounded again.

"That must be the last warning," said Paul hesitantly, looking at Marlene.

"Either that, or a fire drill."

"The last warning," Paul muttered. "I must leave. It's either go now, or wait twenty-seven years for a bridge to be built."

Lou removed the envelope from his pocket and handed it to Paul. "Here you go. You're quite a guy, Frenchie."

Paul took Lou's hand and shook it. "Thank you. Take care of her. Limit her speeches to ten minutes each."

Lou nodded solemnly. Paul faced Marlene, who couldn't bear to look at him.

"No tears," he said. "No sad faces, no remorse, no regrets. . . . We danced as long as the music played. You belong to him now, but you will always be a special part of—" He turned to Lou. "Do I have carbon copies of everything?"

"It's all in there."

"Right," said Paul, as he swiveled back to Marlene. "—a special part of me, and that part will never die. Because to love you is to love a woman, and to love a woman is superior to loving another man, no matter what the poets say. Better, too, than loving other bipeds, and equal almost to loving oneself, provided, of course, that the partner is skilled in foreplay. A woman—"

"Oh, shut your face!" said Marlene.

Paul's shoulders slumped. "You're right. I should go. Even I, DuChard, can not yet walk upon zee water. I've had ideas involving inflatable rubbers, but nothing . . ." He shook his head. *"Au revoir, chérie! Au revoir, monsieur!"*

Suddenly, a voice boomed out of the fog. "Stop where you are, DuChard!"

Schlissel walked forward briskly, a Luger nestled snugly in his palm. The ferry churned and began to pull away.

"Jeezus," said Lou, annoyed. "This case never lets up!"

"If you hadn't been spouting that walk-on-water shit," said Marlene to Paul, "you could've made it, you clod."

Schlissel looked Paul in the eye. "You're coming back to Germany with me, DuChard. I promise you will be given a fair trial and found guilty."

The ferry had moved about two feet from the pier.

"As long as it's a fair trial," said Paul.

Suddenly, Marlene reached forward and grabbed Schlissel's gun hand. "Run, Paul, run!"

Without hesitating, Paul swiveled and broke for the ferry. Schlissel heaved Marlene aside and took careful aim. He bent his knees slightly and used both hands to steady the gun. He had just begun to squeeze the trigger when suddenly a dull thwp! sounded, and he froze dead in his tracks. A neat bullet hole appeared in the exact center of his forehead.

"What a shot!" marveled Lou.

At that instant, Paul leaped from the pier and landed on the deck of the retreating ferry. "A four-foot jump," he called back proudly.

Lieutenant DiMaggio came rushing onto the pier, together with Rizzuto and Crosseti.

"Hello, Frank," said Lou. "I had a hunch you'd follow me down here. D'ja get the other Heinies?"

"They're in the van," said DiMaggio. "And I have this place surrounded. Every man's got a double-barreled shotgun plus a hatpin."

"You won't need them, Frank," said Lou calmly. "I'll handle this. . . ."

He walked over to the next shed. "It's all over, Georgia. You can come out now."

Slowly, Georgia emerged from behind the shed, still dressed in black. In her hands was a gun with a silencer attached. "Hi, Lou. Mad at me?"

Lou's voice was compassionate. "No."

"It was the girl I was trying to shoot. You know how jealous I get."

"I know, kid."

"That's why I killed Floyd. He was getting to spend more time with you than I did."

"We did different things," said Lou.

"I'm sorry about killing all those others in the hotel," continued Georgia. "I must have been irritable."

"Were you pre-menstrual?"

"I think so."

"You shoulda taken some aspirins instead."

"But it's still you and me, isn't it, Lou?" asked Georgia hopefully.

"We'll talk about it, kid."

"With a good lawyer," said Georgia, "I could be out in forty years. I'll watch my weight; I could still be desirable."

"I'm betting on you, kid."

Lou nodded to DiMaggio. Two uniformed policemen took Georgia by the arms.

"Nice night for a boat ride," said Georgia.

Marlene crossed to Lou, and he put his arm around her.

Georgia smiled. "You got yourself one hell of a guy there, lady. If you want to hold onto him, don't burn his bacon."

Marlene smiled and nodded. The cops led Georgia away.

"Can I give you a lift, Lou?" said DiMaggio.

"No thanks, Frank. It's taken care of."

"See you around?"

"Who knows? It's a funny business."

"Yeah," said DiMaggio. He and the other policemen strode away, leaving Lou and Marlene alone.

"Oh, Lou," said Marlene. "We're together. And it's going to be just the way it was, darling."

"No, angel, it's going to be better," said Lou.

220

But his words were drowned out as a large sedan pulled up and screeched to a halt. Hoppy jumped out of the driver's seat.

"I brought the car around, Lou," he said, swatting several giant flies. "Just like you told me to."

"Good boy, Hoppy," said Lou. He opened the rear door, and Marlene climbed in. Lou followed and slammed the door shut. He wriggled his way down into the back seat—not an easy job, since it also held, in addition to Marlene, Betty, Bess, Jezebel, and Mrs. Montenegro.

"Sweetheart," said Lou, "I'd like you to meet the girls. My secretary, Bess, you already know. This is Betty DeBoop, a lot of laughs. Nadia Gladdia Poppenescu, a little kinky, but terrific hands, and, of course, Mrs. . . . uh. . . ."

"Marlene DuChard," said Mrs. Montenegro.

"But I am Marlene DuChard," said Marlene.

"All right," said Mrs. Montenegro. "You'll be Marlene DuChard and I'll be . . . Barbara Stanwyck."

"Nice to meet you," said Marlene. "Hello, girls."

"Let's get outa here, Hoppy," said Lou.

Hoppy started the car. Within a minute, his heavy breathing had eaten away the rear-view mirror.

THE BEST OF THE BESTSELLERS
FROM WARNER BOOKS!

BIG STICK-UP AT BRINK'S!   (81-500, $2.50)
by Noel Behn
Hailed as "the best book about criminals ever written," BRINK'S
recreates a real-life caper more exciting, more engrossing than any
crime novel. It's the most fun you can have from a bank robbery
without taking the money!

PASSION AND PROUD HEARTS   (82-548, $2.25)
by Lydia Lancaster
The sweeping saga of three generations of a family born of a
great love and torn by the hatred between North and South. The
Beddoes family—three generations of Americans joined and divided by love and hate, principle and promise.

SUMMERBLOOD by Anne Rudeen   (82-535, $2.25)
The four exquisite women of Land's End . . . sweet with promise
. . . wild with passion . . . and bound forever to one lonely man
tortured by his terrible past. A big, lush contemporary novel hot
with searing sexuality.

THE FAN by Bob Randall   (82-471, $2.25)
A masterpiece of humor, suspense and terror as an aging Broad-
way actress is pursued by an adoring fan whose obsession with
love and death leads him deeper and deeper into madness. A **New
York Times** bestseller, Literary Guild Alternate, Reader's Digest
Condensed Book, and serialized in **Photoplay.**

THE KINGDOM by Ronald Joseph   (81-467, $2.50)
The saga of a passionate and powerful family who carves out
of the wilderness the largest cattle ranch in the world. Filled
with both adventure and romance, hard-bitten empire building
and tender moments of intimate love, **The Kingdom** is a book
for all readers.

THE BEST OF THE BESTSELLERS
FROM WARNER BOOKS!

IN 1942 THE U.S. RATIONED GASOLINE

The basic ration for passenger cars

A

MILEAGE RATION

A DRIVERS
MUST DISPLAY
THIS STICKER

That was wartime and the spirit of sacrifice was in the air. No one liked it, but everyone went along. Today we need a wartime spirit to solve our energy problems. A spirit of thrift in our use of all fuels, especially gasoline. We Americans pump over 200 million gallons of gasoline into our automobiles each day. That is nearly one-third the nation's total daily oil consumption and more than half of the oil we

import every day . . . at a cost of some $40 billion a year. So conserving gasoline is more than a way to save money at the pump and help solve the nation's balance of payments, it also can tackle a major portion of the nation's energy problem. And that is something we all have a stake in doing . . . with the wartime spirit, but without the devastation of war or the inconvenience of rationing.

ENERGY CONSERVATION - IT'S YOUR CHANCE TO SAVE, AMERICA

Department of Energy, Washington, D.C.

A PUBLIC SERVICE MESSAGE FROM WARNER BOOKS, INC.